MW01615257

DEATH OF A LONG-LOST SON

A gripping British crime mystery full of twists

P.F. FORD

A Slater & Norman Mystery Book 10

Originally published as *A Puzzle of Old Bones*

JOFFE
BOOKS

Revised edition 2024
Joffe Books, London
www.joffebooks.com

First published as *A Puzzle of Old Bones*
in Great Britain in 2017

This paperback edition was first published
in Great Britain in 2024

Cover art by Dee Dee Book Covers

ISBN: 978-1-83526-682-3

To my amazing wife, Mary — sometimes we need someone else to believe in us before we really believe in ourselves. None of this would have happened without her unfailing belief and support.

CHAPTER ONE

Slater eased his car up to the temporary barrier that blocked the road ahead, wound down his window, and showed his warrant card to the bored-looking PC on duty there. The officer made a note on his clipboard and then moved the barrier aside. Slater drove through and headed up the slight incline to the excavation site a hundred yards ahead.

A large white forensics tent had been erected on the right-hand side of the road, covering the verge and ditch alongside it. It served to protect the excavation site not just from the weather, but also from prying eyes — not that there were likely to be many of those out here in the middle of nowhere. That could possibly change once word got out, but so far there were just essential personnel on site and a couple of uniforms manning the barriers.

As Slater approached, a forensically suited-and-booted figure appeared from the far side of the tent and walked out into the road to greet him. It was difficult to recognise anyone in one of those suits, but as he approached, the figure pushed the hood back and shook her head. The dark hair tied in a ponytail was enough to tell Slater who it was before he even saw her face.

He pulled up alongside her, wound down his window, and looked up at her. 'Afternoon, Watson.'

'Afternoon, sir.' Known to all as Watson because of her skills with HOLMES, the police investigative computer system, Detective Sergeant Samantha Brearley was Slater's new sidekick. She stepped back to admire the shiny 4x4 Slater was driving. 'New car, sir?'

He smiled bashfully. 'I thought it was time. That other old thing was on its last legs. I was left some money a while ago and I figured new job, new car, you know? This is more practical than the other thing, and more fitting for a DI, don't you think?'

'I think it's very nice,' she said. 'I love 4x4s.'

'Well, if you behave I might let you sit in the driver's seat later,' said Slater, 'but first, I want to know what we've got here, and what do we know?'

'I assume you know about the tip-off and how they did a search of the area but found no evidence of anything untoward?'

'Yes, Bradshaw told me that much. Exactly how big is this village?'

'If you've just driven through it, you've more or less seen it all, sir. It's little more than a mile from one end to the other, surrounded by fields and not much else.'

'And they didn't find anything,' mused Slater, taking in the surrounding fields. 'Yet here we are, in the middle of October, with a team of experts from MAFU, excavating a dead body.'

'It looks like they missed it,' said Watson. 'But then it *was* at the bottom of a ten-foot-deep ditch.'

Slater continued to look thoughtfully around but said nothing.

'The MAFU people have been working the ditch under the tent,' continued Watson. 'They think they've got all the bones, so the experts are reconstructing the body in their mobile lab while the minions carry on sifting through the site to see if they can find anything else of interest.'

'They're not hanging about then?'

'You know them, don't you, sir?'

'I worked with them once before. Why? Is there a problem?'

Watson paused for a moment. 'Dr Cutter's a bit weird, isn't he?'

Slater laughed as he recalled forensic pathologist Dr Henry Cutter. 'He has a reputation for being something of a maverick,' he said. 'He's very irreverent, likes real ale, likes to listen to really loud rock music when he's working, and the powers-that-be don't like him because he says what he thinks. What's he told you so far?'

'He's being very cagey. He says they're not exactly sure what they've got yet, but he did assure me the bones have been in the ditch for a good few years. I'm sure he knows a lot more than that, but I get the impression he doesn't want to tell me anything.'

'Don't take it personally. As part of Bradshaw's new squad, we're all under close scrutiny,' said Slater. 'Henry's always walking a tightrope anyway, so I suspect he's holding back until he's certain what he's got.'

'Well, if you're sure,' said Watson, sounding unconvinced. 'Maybe he'll tell us a bit more when they've finished the reconstruction.'

'And when will that be?'

'Hopefully later this afternoon.'

'So there's no need to rush then,' said Slater. 'I think it's probably safe to say the culprit's long gone and we've lost the element of surprise.'

'That's rather what I thought, sir,' she agreed. 'So, if it's all right with you, I'll jump in next to you and show you where I've set up camp before we do anything else.'

She walked around the car and climbed into the passenger seat. 'Oh gosh, this is nice,' she said as she settled back into the leather upholstery.

'Camp? Did you say camp?' asked a dismayed Slater. 'We're not working in a tent, are we?'

'Good heavens, no, sir,' she said. 'It's much better than that.' She pointed the way ahead. 'Come on, I'll show you. It's just up here.'

Slater set off along the road, which began to bend to the left. As the road straightened out again, Watson pointed to the right. 'Take the turning off to the right, just there.'

'I'm not taking my new car into a ploughed field!' Slater spluttered as he turned off the road onto a farm track.

Watson turned to look at him. 'I thought that was the whole point of a 4x4.'

'Well, yeah, but only if it's really necessary!' he replied.

'You needn't worry, sir, we're not going across any fields,' she said with a little grin. 'Just follow the track and then turn to the right again, just here.'

He swung the car to the right and followed the new track up to the top of a rise. As he reached the top, Slater stopped. A large barn, which had been hidden behind the rise, was now fully visible. It was open on three sides, with just one solid wall facing across the fields to serve as weather protection. As they approached, Slater could see two vehicles were parked under the barn. One, Slater recognised as the enormous articulated truck that served as the MAFU (Mobile Autonomous Forensic Unit) mobile lab. The other, parked alongside, was slightly smaller.

'There you are — home sweet home,' said Watson.

Slater turned to her. 'Did you organise all this?'

'It was a bit of luck really, sir,' she said as he drove down to the barn. 'MAFU needed somewhere to park that monster truck of theirs, and we needed somewhere for ours, and the barn was empty, so I found the farmer and asked him. He was very amenable when I told him what we wanted it for.'

They had reached the barn now and Slater stopped the car. The track they were on ran parallel to the road, and they were almost exactly opposite the excavation site. A massive pile of soil off to one side showed someone had recently bull-dozed a path from the barn to the site.

'We thought it might be easier if we could approach from the side of the ditch,' explained Watson. 'I managed to sweet-talk the farmer into letting Dr Cutter borrow his JCB and move a bit of soil out of the way.'

Watson waited, drumming her fingers on the dashboard, as Slater sat and took it all in. 'What do you think?' she burst out at last.

'I'll tell you what I think,' he said, slowly. 'I think it's as close to perfect as we could possibly have asked for. And I think you're pretty amazing for having the gumption to get it organised.'

Watson blushed. 'Well, thank you, sir, but I was only doing my job.'

'I think you underestimate yourself,' Slater said. 'This is way beyond just doing your job.'

Watson beamed. 'You haven't seen inside our mobile office, have you? We've even got a small kitchen so we can make tea and coffee and the odd snack. Come on, I'll show you, I'm gasping for a cup of tea.'

She jumped from the car and led him down the side of their truck and up a small set of steps to the door of their office.

'Of course, we're out in the middle of nowhere,' she said, as she opened the door and ushered him inside, 'but that's not a problem as we've got satellite broadband through a dish on the roof, and there's a small generator for power.' She opened a door at one end and walked through. 'There's a tiny kitchen in here and a loo opposite.'

Slater listened to her filling the kettle and switching it on as he took in the office. The space was small, but whoever had designed the interior had managed to fit desktops all around the walls with working spaces at each end. It was a purpose-built office for two.

'What about the rest of the team?' he called out to her.

Watson stood in the doorway as she waited for the kettle to boil. 'They're back at base. All we have to do is let them know and they'll do any research we need.'

'You seem to have thought of everything. Do we have room service?'

Watson looked confused. 'I'm sorry, sir, I'm not with you.'

'Relax, Watson, it's just a joke.' Slater reached into his pocket, found one of his new business cards, and handed it to her. 'The boss tells me you're responsible for this.'

Watson looked at the card and then up at Slater. 'I'm sorry, sir, is there a problem?'

'It says DI David Slater. I haven't been called David since I was a little boy.'

'Oh, right, I see.' Watson sounded rather crestfallen. 'Actually, I thought David sounded more dignified.'

'More dignified?'

'Yes. I know you have to go through this twelve-month probationary thing, but you're the boss now, so you want to be taken seriously, don't you? Dave sounds like one of the boys, maybe even a bit of a lad, whereas David sounds much more like the boss. I think Detective Inspector David Slater sounds like you mean business. It has a lot more gravitas, don't you agree?'

Slater pursed his lips. 'More *gravitas*?'

'Do you do that a lot?' asked Watson, failing to disguise the irritation in her voice.

Slater turned away and smiled to himself. 'Do what a lot?'

'Repeat what I say as a question. That's three times now in a matter of seconds. It's quite annoying, and if you don't mind me saying, if you're doing it on purpose, it's beneath your dignity, sir.'

Slater suppressed a laugh. 'Ah, yes, I must preserve my dignity.'

Watson frowned. 'Look, if the cards bother you that much, I can change the name and have them printed again.'

'And lose all my gravitas?' said Slater, his grin widening as he turned to face her. 'I don't think so.'

'Well, what *do* you want, sir?' asked Watson, sounding exasperated. 'Perhaps a bit of guidance at this stage might prevent me continuing to get things so wrong.'

Slater studied her face for a couple of seconds before he spoke. 'What I want, Watson, is for you to lighten up a bit. I'm quite happy with the cards, I was just teasing.'

A faint blush crept onto her cheeks.

'I know you want to make a good impression, but believe me, you're not on trial here,' he continued, 'and, as far as I can see, you haven't done anything wrong. Look what you've done with this mobile office set-up. You've even managed to find a building big enough to provide shelter from the weather for two trucks, one of which is enormous. How many people do you think could have done that?

'You got this job because I wanted someone I could trust and rely on. You proved your value when you were working with me before, that's why I insisted you should be my DS if I took this job.'

Watson's blush began to deepen in colour. 'You did? Gosh!'

'Well, don't sound so surprised. I did say you would be my first choice as long as you passed the medical. So how is the bionic knee?'

'Yes, sir, sorry, sir, the knee is "A one", sir.'

'Yes, I guessed as much from the absence of your walking stick.' Slater studied her for a moment. 'Remind me about your history, Watson. I seem to recall you are ex-military?'

'I was in the Royal Military Police before I joined the police force.'

Slater nodded. 'Aha! Now that explains a lot. Okay, so you want a bit of guidance to help you work with me? Then here it is. You'll have noticed we don't go around stamping our feet and saluting all the time. That's because "A" we don't want to hurt our feet and "B" we're the police, not the military. That second bit also means you don't have to stand to attention when I'm speaking to you.'

Watson visibly relaxed. It was obvious she hadn't even realised she had been standing so rigidly.

'We're a two-person team,' continued Slater, 'and in my opinion, that team will work best when both partners are comfortable and relaxed. So, which do you prefer: Sam or Samantha?'

'I prefer Sam to Samantha,' she said, 'but if it's all the same to you, sir, I've rather got used to being Watson.'

'Whatever works for you is fine by me,' said Slater.

'Yes, sir, thank you, sir.'

Slater shook his head. 'Now, that's something that I'm not comfortable with.'

Watson looked puzzled. 'What's that, sir?'

'All that "yes sir, no sir stuff". Like I said, you're not in the army now. I appreciate there are some occasions where we need to be formal, but when it's just the two of us I don't see the need.'

'But Mr Bradshaw—'

'You don't work for Bradshaw any more, Watson. You work for me.'

'But I can't call you Dave or David, sir, that just wouldn't be right.'

'Okay, so, what would be right?' he asked, patiently.

'Well, "sir" would be fine for me, but if you're not happy with that, I understand the norm is to use "guv" or "boss".'

Slater smiled broadly. 'Somehow, Watson, I don't see you as a "guv" sort of girl.'

Watson's blush had almost faded away to nothing, but now it came glowing back again. Slater hadn't intended to embarrass her, so he was quick to move on. 'Look, I know the way I work is new to you, and I'm sure you're going to find I've got some very irritating habits. I'm also reasonably confident we're going to have the odd disagreement until we get used to each other, but that's the nature of any relationship. The thing is, I don't want you tiptoeing around worrying about that. We'll work out how to cross that particular bridge when, or if, we come to it. In the meantime, I just want you to relax, be yourself, do your job, and try to enjoy yourself. I know it's a grim business a lot of the time, but that doesn't mean we can't see the funny side. It's how a lot of people cope, like Henry Cutter, and it works for me, too, so don't be surprised if I'm not deadly serious all the time. Okay?'

Watson smiled at last. 'Yes, I remember that,' she said. 'I don't know if I said at the time, but I actually enjoyed working with you and Mr Norman very much. It was quite different to what I'm used to.'

Slater smiled fondly. 'Yeah, it's difficult not to enjoy working with Norm.'

'He's certainly not one for formalities, is he?'

'And that's exactly the sort of atmosphere I work best in,' said Slater, 'so let's see if we can keep it like that.'

'I'll do my best,' said Watson.

'Just relax, and you'll be fine.'

CHAPTER TWO

Shortly after four p.m., Slater reintroduced himself to Dr Henry Cutter and his tiny forensic anthropologist partner Dr Nadira, so-called because of her almost unpronounceable surname. They spent five minutes on shared reminiscences about the last time they were on a case together, and then it was time to discuss the problem lurking under a sheet before them.

'There was a time when I would have reported this straight away,' confessed Cutter, 'but we wanted to be absolutely sure, so we've basically been sitting on our evidence and hedging our bets.'

'I thought Bradshaw was a bit vague,' said Slater.

'Our little unit would have been disbanded if it wasn't for Bradshaw, so we owe him. There are still plenty of people who would like to see him fail, so we don't want to flag up something that might later prove to be mistaken.' Cutter turned to Watson. 'That's why I've a been a bit cagey with you. I hope you'll forgive me.'

Watson looked surprised to hear Cutter's apology, but she nodded her assent. 'Of course.'

'But you think you can tell us what's what now?' asked Slater.

Cutter nodded to his tiny colleague, and she removed the sheet to reveal the skeleton. He looked up at Slater as a groan of dismay escaped his lips. 'That's right.' Cutter sighed. 'You don't need to be an expert to see it's the skeleton of a child — a young boy in fact.'

'I could see it wasn't a giant, but I was hoping it might just be a small woman,' muttered Slater, his disappointment loud and clear. Watson looked equally disturbed.

'We're checking dental records, and we've taken DNA samples from the teeth, but even though I made it high priority, the results will take a couple of days to come back,' said Cutter. 'And unless there's someone on the database who's a match, even that won't be a lot of help.'

'At least if we can find possible parents we'll be able to make a start,' said Slater. 'What else do you know? Can you tell us how old he was when he died?'

'The growth of bones is a pretty good indicator,' said Nadira, 'and teeth can tell us a lot, too. I can't tell you his exact age yet, but I believe he was somewhere between five and eight years old. I've asked for much more detailed analysis to be more accurate, but that could take a couple of weeks.'

Watson and Slater exchanged a look. 'Can you tell us anything about how he died?' asked Slater.

'That's not clear-cut,' said Nadira. 'There are no obvious damage marks anywhere on the skeleton, although the hyoid bone is fractured which suggests—'

'Strangulation.' Watson's voice was almost a whisper.

'That's very good,' said Nadira. 'If it was an adult I'd say it was almost a certainty, but it's not as reliable an indicator of strangulation in children. I'd say it's a strong possibility, but I couldn't say for sure.'

'But if you had to put money on it?' asked Slater.

'A bit better than evens,' said Cutter.

'Okay.' Slater took a deep breath. 'So we have a little boy, six or seven years old, who may have been strangled.'

'It's not much to go on, but I can start searching for missing boys who fit the description,' said Watson. 'Can you tell us how long ago he died?'

'At this stage, I would estimate he's been in the ground anything from five to fifteen years,' said Nadira. 'Again, I can be a lot more precise when we've had more time.'

'At least we've got somewhere to start.' Watson's voice sounded determined.

'Yes, thanks, guys, that's great work,' said Slater. 'It's just a pity you had to spoil our day in the process.'

'It tends to go with the territory, I'm afraid,' said Cutter, with a rueful smile. 'We're hoping we will be able to tell you more tomorrow. We've got more stuff we dug out of the ditch to go through yet. Perhaps we'll get lucky and find something to identify him.'

'Yeah, a name and address would be good,' said Slater, smiling back sadly.

'If only we could,' said Cutter. 'We'll see what we can do, starting in the morning. Right now, we're going to shut down for the day.'

CHAPTER THREE

'They have a very strange set-up,' said Watson, turning her chair around to face Slater across the office.

Slater had been idly swivelling his chair from side to side, but now he laughed. 'They like working with dead bodies. In my book that makes them strange people.'

'Yes, but even so,' said Watson, doubtfully.

'Strange in what way?'

'Well, where do they sleep, for a start. Are they in the lab with dead bodies? And where do they shower?'

'They've got a shower in the lab. They have to have those facilities in their line of work. And have you seen the size of the cab on that wagon of theirs? It's got a sleeping compartment up behind the driver. I should imagine it's pretty cosy.'

'But where does the other one sleep?'

Slater looked at Watson and gave her a sympathetic smile. Was she really that naive? 'Like I said, I should imagine it's pretty cosy in that sleeping compartment.' He finished with a theatrical wink.

Watson looked shocked. 'You mean . . . Gosh! Really?'

'Like rabbits,' said Slater, enjoying himself hugely.

Now Watson was blushing a nice shade of crimson. 'Is that even allowed?'

'Probably not,' said Slater. 'But I told you — Henry's a maverick. Personally, I don't care what he and Nadira get up to in their own time as long as they do their job.' He looked at his watch. 'Are we booked into a hotel? Is it far away?'

'It's a small family-run place. It's only ten minutes away.'

'Okay, we're both staying in the hotel, there's nothing to rush home for, so how about we have a quick planning meeting now and get ourselves ready to start in earnest first thing tomorrow?'

'That's fine by me,' said Watson.

'So, you tell me, where should we start?' Slater suppressed a smile as Watson's cheeks glowed pink slightly. He got the impression that almost every boss she had worked with before had treated her more like a gofer. When he'd worked with her on a case a few months previously, she had seemed shocked when he had valued her opinion and even asked for it.

'Well, at the moment we have no idea who he is, so we can't go down the obvious route,' she said. 'But maybe we can start from the other end and find a missing person's report that fits our victim. If I go back fifteen years, do you think that will be enough?'

Slater felt slightly frustrated at the lack of direct actions they could actually take, but nodded. 'I feel we should be doing more but, quite frankly, that's about all we can do right now.'

'I know what you mean,' said Watson. 'In normal cases there are usually clues you can act upon more or less immediately, and forensic evidence to work with, but with these old cases it's a very different situation.'

'You're telling me. When I made that comment about the culprit being long gone, I didn't realise just how true that was. Right now we literally have no idea what we're dealing with or where to start.'

Watson swung her chair round and began tapping away at her laptop. Slater sat and contemplated for a couple of minutes, still swinging his chair from side to side. This was frustrating, but really, what more could they do? 'Are you busy, Watson?'

'Just setting up this search,' she called over her shoulder. 'It'll only take a couple of minutes.'

'When you've finished we might as well call it a day and go and check in to that hotel.'

Five minutes later, Watson closed her laptop, packed it away in its case, and swung her chair round to face him. 'Ready when you are, boss.'

He threw his car keys to her. 'You can drive.'

'Really? But it's your new car!'

'I did say you could sit in the driver's seat if you behaved yourself.'

'Yes, but it's new.'

'You can drive, can't you?'

'Well, yes. But what about my car?'

'It'll be safe enough here. What's the point in us taking two cars over to the hotel, and then driving them both back again tomorrow? Think green, Watson.'

'I suppose you have a point,' she conceded. 'If you're sure.'

'I am, so come on, let's go.'

CHAPTER FOUR

'You knew I was going to be staying away as long as this case lasted.' Slater readjusted his mobile phone into a more comfortable position. 'It's just not practical for me to spend four or five hours driving every day. We agreed we would find somewhere to live once I'm working from my new base.'

Much as Slater adored his girlfriend, Jenny, if there was one thing he didn't like about her, it was her ability to sulk like a spoilt child when it suited her. He knew for a fact that if he could see her face right now, she would be pouting like a five-year-old and quite possibly stamping her feet like one too.

'But I'm on my own, it's not fair,' she whined.

'But you knew it was going to be like this,' argued Slater. 'I went over it again and again to make sure you understood. You're the one who kept telling me how you were fed up having me watching you all the time. Well, now you've got the freedom you craved, right?'

'Yes, but—'

'You wanted me to take this job. Didn't you tell me I'd be a fool not to take it?'

'Well, yes, but—'

'You can't have it both ways, Jenny. I'm here now, and I'm staying here until this case is closed.'

'How do I know I can trust what's-her-name?'

'D'you mean Watson?' Slater asked, incredulously. 'What makes you think she's remotely interested in me? Are you telling me you don't trust me?'

'Of course not.'

'Well, that's what it sounds like.'

'But she's a very good-looking girl.'

'The world's full of good-looking girls, but that doesn't mean I'm trying to climb into bed with all of them, does it?'

'But you're not working closely with all of them, and I bet you're in the same hotel.'

'Of course we're in the same hotel, but we're not in the same damned room, are we?' he asked, exasperated. 'Jesus, Jen, what's got into you?'

'I'm stuck here in this boring one-horse town, and I'm lonely, that's all.'

'It was a good enough town when you were in trouble and looking for help,' he reminded her.

'That was different.'

'Anyway, I thought you liked your own company,' Slater said, soothingly.

'Well, yes I do, but I'd rather have you here. I need you here.'

'Well, I'm sorry, but you're just going to have to make do for now.'

'Well, poo to you,' she said. 'I won't talk to you if you're going to be like that.' And with that, she hung up.

Slater looked accusingly at his phone, muttered a curse, and shut his phone down. Women. He wondered if he would ever really understand them, then decided that no, of course he wouldn't. He found the TV remote control and started to scroll through the channels to find something to watch. If Jenny wanted to sulk, she would just have to get on with it. He wasn't going to play that game.

CHAPTER FIVE

It was seven thirty when Slater and Watson met in the dining room for breakfast. At seven thirty-five, Watson's mobile phone pinged. 'We've got some results from my search,' she said. 'They've sent me an email. It'll be waiting when we get to the office.'

Before Slater could answer, his own phone began to ring. 'Henry's got some more information for us,' he told Watson when he hung up. 'He'll be waiting for us when we get on-site.'

Just over half an hour later they were back on site, standing in the MAFU mobile lab. Looking at the state of Henry Cutter, it was obvious he had had little — or no — sleep the previous night. Nadira looked as serene as always, but Slater was pretty sure she was one of those people who would always look the same whatever happened.

'Have you two been working all night?' he asked.

Cutter looked a little sheepish, and for the briefest moment Slater thought he was going to confess to the cause of his bleary eyes being something that would surely shock Watson. But he nodded.

'Okay,' Slater said, 'so tell me what's so important you needed to disturb my breakfast?'

'Well, we appreciate you need something concrete to get started and, frankly, we felt we didn't give you that yesterday,' explained Cutter. 'We also fancy a day off, so we thought we could kill two birds with one stone if we worked late last night and find you something to be going on with.'

Watson looked sceptically across at Slater. He winked back at her. 'And did you find us something?'

'Let's say we can take the rest of today off without having to carry a guilty conscience around,' said Cutter. 'Last night we decided to go through all the other stuff we had dug up to see if we could find something that would help you. I must stress that we still need the results from more detailed analysis to be one hundred per cent sure of our findings, but even without that, we're ninety per cent sure we're correct.'

'Okay, let's hear it then,' said Slater.

'Going on the rate of decomposition of natural and man-made fibres, it's possible to deduce how long something has been underground. Likewise, you can do much the same with bones. There is a margin of error, of course, but because of these additional factors, we're able to narrow the time of the burial down to somewhere between six and ten years.'

'We've also got a couple of bits and pieces that may help with identification,' said Nadira. 'These were found within the vicinity of the body, so we're confident they belong to the victim.'

Cutter produced several clear plastic bags and placed them on the table. 'We've got some sort of plastic doll, in remarkably good condition, some fabric remnants from the boy's clothing, although it's hard to decide what colour they might have been when he was wearing them, two leather shoes with rubber soles that are hopefully in good enough condition to be identifiable, and then we have the pièce de résistance.' He produced one more, much smaller, plastic bag and placed it before Slater and Watson.

'Oh my goodness,' said Watson.

'Wow!' said Slater. 'Now that really could help.'

'I thought you'd like it,' said Cutter. 'We think it's perhaps a Christening gift, or something similar.'

Slater picked up the bag and studied the contents, then he passed it to Watson. 'Not just any old St Christopher pendant,' he muttered. 'It looks a bit special, doesn't it?'

'Maybe it was specially made,' said Watson.

'There is a hallmark,' said Cutter. 'It's pretty worn and faded, but we looked at it under the microscope and we're pretty sure it's the mark of Edmond Moynihan. He was a Dublin silversmith working in the late 1800s. Having said that, I'm no expert in these things so you'll need to check that out.'

'This could be really important in narrowing our search,' said Slater. 'There can't be that many missing kids with an antique, sterling silver pendant round their neck.'

CHAPTER SIX

Slater carefully added the information they had gathered so far to the whiteboard that took up one wall of the office. He stepped back to admire his handiwork and pulled a gloomy face. There wasn't exactly what he would call a lot to go on. The only thing they knew for sure was the date of the tip-off that had led them to the skeleton, which was written in the top left-hand corner. This was accompanied by an aerial photo of the location, a photo of the skeleton in situ, another of the skeleton laid out on a table in the MAFU lab, and photos of the other items that had been found in the grave. A Post-it note that read: *Buried six–ten years ago* had been stuck alongside the photos, and that was about it.

'Goodness,' said Watson's voice from behind him. She was staring at the email she had just opened. 'I've seen the statistics, but they don't seem to mean anything when you look at them from a distance.'

'What's up?' asked Slater.

There was a heavy sigh. 'I suppose I had no idea so many children went missing every year.'

'It's frightening, isn't it? But try not to dwell on the numbers, or it will depress the hell out of you. You can't deal with them all, so keep a bit of distance and focus on the ones that might be relevant to our case.'

'There must be almost a hundred names on this list,' she said, gloomily.

'They can't all be in the right age range,' said Slater. He peered over her shoulder and studied the email. Then he pointed over her shoulder. 'Look, it says they've extended the search parameters.'

'I don't see how that makes the situation any better for all these kids.'

'It doesn't,' said Slater, gently, 'but we can only deal with one at a time. And right now, we need to focus on the one who's lying on a table in that lab next door.'

'Yes, boss, I'm sorry.'

He moved to one side and leaned back against the desktop so he could see her face. 'I take it you've not dealt with many missing children.'

'Not one,' she admitted, looking up at him. 'I guess I've been lucky so far.'

'You certainly have. I'm afraid now it's a case of "welcome to the real world", but at least we already know what's happened to the boy. Finding a body when you're looking for a live one is far worse, trust me.'

'I'm sorry,' said Watson, guiltily. 'That was rather unprofessional of me.'

'Don't worry about it,' said Slater, with a reassuring smile, 'and don't ever be ashamed of showing your humanity. If you weren't affected by it, I'd think there was something wrong with you. You just have to try not to focus on it.'

'Right. I'll try.'

'Why don't you send a copy of that list across to me? You start from the top and I'll start from the bottom.'

* * *

An hour later, they had managed to narrow their list down to just five possibilities. Watson then spent another hour searching out further information through the central database.

'I think number forty-eight on the list looks the strongest candidate,' she said. 'Sonny Randall. He was six years old when he was reported missing on 22 October 2006. It says here he was wearing a silver pendant when he went missing. The parents live in a village called Flipton Dene.'

'How far's that?' asked Slater.

'Well, Flipton's a hundred miles away, and the village is about five miles further on.'

'Before we go charging up there, I'd better speak to Bradshaw. Maybe he can break the ice with the Flipton police and let them know we think we might have found their missing kid from ten years ago. Maybe he can persuade them to let us have their case file.'

CHAPTER SEVEN

Chief Superintendent Bradshaw had told them the person they needed to speak to was DCI Charlie Lipton, but he was proving to be a hard man to get hold of, and Slater had been holding for a good ten minutes before he heard the sounds of life at the other end of the phone.

'Hello?' said a voice at last.

'DCI Lipton? This is DI Slater.'

'Yes, Superintendent Bradshaw told me you'd be calling. What can I do for you, Slater? Bradshaw said you'd uncovered a child's body. What makes you think it's got anything to do with us?'

'Our forensic pathology people have told us the body was buried between six and ten years ago. We've looked at every unsolved missing child case from that period, and the one that seems to fit the bill is Sonny Randall. He went mi—'

'I don't need you to tell me when he went missing, Slater,' said Lipton, testily. 'It's not something I'm ever likely to forget, is it?'

'Yes, sir, sorry, sir.'

'So, what have you found?'

'The child was wearing a pendant. According to the notes I've seen, it looks like we might have a match. I was wondering if I was to send you a photograph, would you be able to identify it?'

'No, I can't do that,' said Lipton.

Slater was a bit taken aback by the abruptness of Lipton's response. He had known there was a good chance Lipton wouldn't be keen on helping them, and he could understand. No one liked handing a case on to someone else, it was like admitting you had failed. Even so, he was rather disappointed. If he had to go back to Bradshaw and ask him to intervene, it would mean using someone up high to lean on Lipton, and it was unlikely that would lead to cordial relations. The last thing they needed was a turf war. He would have to be careful how he handled this.

'I can hear you thinking,' said Lipton's voice in his ear. 'You think I'm going to make life difficult for you, don't you?'

'Err, well, I do understand,' said Slater. 'No one wants to hand a case over to someone else.'

Lipton laughed — a mirthless laugh. 'Actually, Slater, I can't tell you about the pendant because we have no photo and only a cursory description. I can assure you I have no problem handing this case over to you. We're up to our necks here, and I don't actually have the manpower to reopen that case, so you're welcome to it. If you give me a couple of hours, I'll get someone to copy the file and email it to you.'

Slater couldn't quite believe his luck, but he knew there must be more to this than met the eye, and he wondered what Lipton wasn't telling him. 'We want to come up and speak to the parents tomorrow,' he said. 'Why don't we call in and pick the file up?'

'How big's the boot of your car?' asked Lipton.

'The file's a bit big, is it?'

'Massive.'

'Err, can I ask a question, sir?'

'Go ahead.'

'Is there anything else I should know about this case?'

Lipton laughed more easily this time. 'There are no flies on you, are there, Slater?'

'I just get the feeling—'

'Well, since you're sharp enough to spot it, and ask,' said Lipton, 'I'll warn you. The problem is the parents, Alan and Diana Randall. They are, shall we say, not the most helpful people I've ever had to deal with. Diana was once a DI herself, and she thinks she's the only one who knows how to run an investigation.'

'Ah, great.' Slater heaved a sigh. 'There's nothing like an ex-copper to hinder an investigation.'

'And she will hinder you,' said Lipton. 'I always felt she knew more than she was letting on, but I could never prove anything. My advice would be to tread very carefully, but even if you do, I expect she'll be calling me to complain about you.'

'Terrific,' said Slater. 'I'll look forward to a bollocking from you.'

CHAPTER EIGHT

The village of Flipton Dene was one of those idyllic English rural villages with a duck pond, a beautiful old church, a classic country pub, and even a village green with a cricket square in the middle. The properties around the central, original part of the village were suitably ancient, many with thatched roofs. These were interspersed with a few rather grand Georgian houses, a number of Victorian homes, and a splendid old rectory.

At the northern end of the village, the twentieth century had insinuated itself into the surroundings — first with the unwelcome addition of an estate of characterless prefabricated boxes, and then later with some rather attractive homes more in sympathy with the countryside in which they were located. It was at this end of the village, down a neat, tidy lane, that the Randalls lived.

'Nice house,' remarked Slater as they pulled up in the lane outside. 'What did you say this guy does?'

'Some sort of climate scientist,' replied Watson. 'He's written loads of books, articles and reports on climate change. He even has his own newspaper column in one of the Sundays.'

'Nice work if you can get it.'

* * *

'I've been expecting you, please come in,' said Mr Randall abruptly, stepping back and swinging the door open. He was tall and rangy, with piercing blue eyes. His hair was greying at the temples, but he had a full head of still-dark hair. If anything gave his age away, it was his craggy face, convincing Slater he must be at least sixty. He had been expecting someone younger.

Randall led them through to a large, comfortable lounge and indicated a large settee. 'Please sit down. My wife will join us in a minute. As you can imagine, this has been a bit of a shock for her after all this time.'

'Yes, I can understand that,' said Slater. 'I'm only sorry we're not here with good news.'

'You have to hope for the best,' said Randall, his face a picture of tragedy. 'Although having been in the police, Diana knew the statistics. She told me at the end of the first week that we were unlikely to ever see our son again.'

It seemed to Slater that Alan Randall was still living through the agony of losing his son. He almost felt embarrassed to be watching. Then, Diana Randall glided through the door, and Slater and Watson stood up. She was the picture of elegance and oozed composure. If she was upset, she certainly didn't show it.

She greeted them with a smile. 'Good morning, sorry to keep you waiting.'

Alan Randall did the introductions and they all shook hands.

'Do sit down, please,' said Diana, suddenly all business-like. 'We all know why you're here, and I know from my own experience you'd rather be almost anywhere else, so let's cut to the chase and get this over with.'

Slater was slightly taken aback by her attitude. It didn't match the impression Alan Randall's comments had created, but then again, how did anyone face up to a situation like this? Everyone handled it in a different way, and who was he to judge?

'Okay,' he said, 'I'll try not to prolong this any longer than I have to. The fact is, we've found a body, and we believe it may be your son.'

'How long has this body been in the ground?'

Slater felt rather uncomfortable.

'Come now, Inspector Slater,' said Diana. 'I assume you know I was a DI myself once, so I know how this goes. You don't have to use tippy-toes with me. I'm just trying to make it easier for all of us.'

'Yes, of course.' Slater was irritated with himself now. 'The forensic pathologist believes he's been there between six and ten years.'

Alan Randall let out a little gasp, but Diana ignored him. 'What makes you so sure it's my son?' she asked. 'Surely there can't be much left if he's been in there that long.'

'We're not one hundred per cent sure it is him,' admitted Slater, 'but we've managed to salvage some items that we believe are his. There's this doll.' He passed the first photograph across to her.

Diana looked down at the photograph, then back up at Slater. 'This doesn't prove anything. They must have sold millions of those dolls. Almost every little boy on the planet had one.'

Slater passed her a second photograph. 'How about these shoes?'

Diana glanced at the photo and then rolled her eyes as she turned back to Slater. 'It's a pair of shoes.'

'Okay,' said Slater, more patiently than he felt, 'what about this?' He handed the photograph of the pendant to her.

She looked down at the photograph just as she had the others, but this time she took a bit longer. Slater watched as her fingers whitened where she gripped the photograph. She swallowed hard as she looked up at him. 'This doesn't prove anything.'

'When you first reported your son missing, you mentioned a St Christopher pendant, and even though you didn't give a very thorough description, you did say it was a family piece,' said Watson. 'We think the pendant we have found matches the description you gave, and your son's was the only unsolved case where the missing child was wearing a pendant.'

Diana looked at Watson as if she had just crawled from the nearest gutter. 'If you ever lose a child of your own,' she snapped, 'you'll find it's not very easy to think clearly about something as trivial as a pendant. I also think I deserve the courtesy of being spoken to by an officer of equal rank, don't you?'

'I'm sorry,' said Slater, bristling. 'We must have been misinformed. I thought you were no longer in the force.'

'I left fourteen years ago.' She sniffed.

'Which means you don't actually have a rank,' said Slater. 'You're not being interviewed under caution, and my sergeant is only doing her job, which, as you said earlier, is a job neither of us want to do.'

Diana Randall's eyes flashed angrily as she glared at Slater for a moment and then she let out a sigh. 'I'm sorry,' she said, eventually, 'but this is a very stressful situation for me. Can you imagine what it's like to have two complete strangers come into your house and tell you they've found your son's body? It would be bad enough, but you're not even sure, are you?'

'But the pendant—'

'There are probably dozens of them about,' said Diana, her voice beginning to rise. 'It doesn't prove anything!'

All the time they had been speaking, Alan Randall had sat to one side, almost as if he didn't belong there.

'What about you, Mr Randall?' asked Slater.

'He's obviously in shock,' said Diana, before her husband could speak. 'Have you no sympathy? He's only going to say the same as me anyway.'

Slater thought Alan Randall certainly appeared to be at a loss, but he wasn't convinced shock had anything to do with it. 'Would you be willing to provide DNA samples?' he asked. 'That way we would know for sure.'

'I don't think so,' said Diana. 'I've already told you it's not my son. DNA will only confirm that.'

'Isn't that what you want?'

'No,' she said, adamantly, raising her voice to a screech. 'It's what you want. I already know it's not my son!'

'Yes, but—' began Slater, but her screeching voice seemed to have galvanised Alan Randall into life.

'I think it's time you left now,' he said, getting to his feet. 'How dare you come here upsetting my wife like this?'

'It only takes a minute to get a sample,' said Slater.

'Get out of my house, now!'

CHAPTER NINE

'And that, Watson, is a lesson in how not to handle an interview,' said Slater as they drove away from the Randall's house.

'I'm sorry if I spoke out of turn in there,' she said.

'You didn't, it was a perfectly fair question.'

'Well, thank you for defending me, but I think the interview went rapidly downhill from there onwards, so I feel it was my fault.'

'Diana Randall was the reason the interview went downhill,' said Slater grimly. 'She obviously thinks she's something special, when she isn't.' He sighed in exasperation. 'What a way to start my twelve-month probationary period as a DI. I've never had an interview go that bad. I made a right pig's ear of it.'

'To be fair, sir, I don't think Mrs Randall had any intention of admitting we've found her son. And didn't you find it a bit strange that Mr Randall hardly said a word? It was almost as if he was there, but he wasn't, if you see what I mean.'

'It was a bit weird, wasn't it? But then so was her attitude. She clearly recognised that pendant, but then denied it could be hers.'

'Perhaps she just doesn't want to face the truth and admit her son's dead,' suggested Watson.

'There is another possibility,' said Slater. 'Maybe I'm jumping to conclusions, but it's possible she's denying this is her son because she knows for sure that she's right.'

'But she could only know that if she knew—'

'Exactly,' said Slater. 'She could only know this isn't her son if she knew for sure where her son actually was.'

'D'you really think she could have murdered her own son?' asked Watson.

'She wouldn't be the first mother to do it. Suppose she had given up her career and left the force because of him? Maybe she came to resent it so much . . .'

'What if it was both of them?'

'Alan Randall doesn't look as if he's got it in him, but he knows a lot more than he's saying, that's for sure.'

'They didn't seem like a happy couple, did they?' said Watson, thoughtfully.

'She's a strange one that's for sure,' said Slater. 'I can't imagine her as a detective. She's far too feminine.'

Watson gave him a sideways look. 'Why, thank you, sir,' she said frostily. 'Should I take that as a compliment or an insult?'

'What?' Slater realised what he'd said. 'No. Wait. That didn't come out right. What I mean is—'

'I can assure you I can do feminine. I can glam up any time I want, but I wouldn't be much use at work if I came in wearing a little black dress, killer heels, and worrying I might chip my nail varnish now, would I?'

'I'm quite sure you can do feminine whenever you want,' said Slater hastily, 'but that's exactly my point. Diana Randall doesn't look the sort who can un-glam, if you see what I mean. She'd be too worried about her immaculate appearance to want to get her hands dirty at work. Whereas you take the practical approach and dress appropriately for the job.'

He stared straight ahead, avoiding her gaze, hoping he'd done enough to get his point over and put things right. They drove on in silence for a few minutes before he spoke again.

'Are we good?' he asked, looking across at her. 'You know I didn't mean to offend you, don't you?'

'D'you know,' she said, focusing on the road ahead, 'you are the strangest boss I have ever worked for.'

'What's that supposed to mean?'

'Well, for a start you ask for my opinion. That's hard enough to understand. Then you took my side against Diana Randall, and now you're worried that you might have offended me.'

'I value your opinion, Watson, because two heads are better than one. And there's no way I'm going to sit there and let someone speak to you like that woman did. And I am worried I might have offended you because it wasn't my intention.'

'But you're the boss.'

'That doesn't make me right all the time, and it certainly doesn't give me the right to insult you.'

Now Watson was smiling. 'No offence taken, honestly, boss. If anything, I'm rather flattered to find you have such a high opinion of me. There is one thing I'd like to ask, though?'

'Go on.'

'Can we stop somewhere and have a coffee? I'm gasping.'

Now Slater smiled too. 'You're driving. Stop wherever you like. I think we've earned it.'

* * *

Watson took a long sip of coffee and let out a sigh of satisfaction. She looked over at Slater; she was glad he hadn't taken offence earlier when she'd told him he was the strangest boss she had worked for.

'So how old do you think Diana Randall is?' Slater asked her.

She thought for a moment. 'Mid to late forties. He's a lot older than her.'

'That's what I thought,' said Slater. 'So let's guess at forty-eight. That means if she left the force fourteen years ago she would have been, what, thirty-four years old?'

'Must have been about that,' agreed Watson, wondering where Slater was going with this.

'Yet she was already a DI and had been for four years. She must have been a bit special.'

'I suppose.' Watson was thirty-four herself and had worked damned hard to get to DS, so Diana Randall must have been something special.

'Now, why would someone like that walk away from her career at such a young age? Doesn't that strike you as a bit odd?'

'A baby?'

'There was no sign of anyone young in that house, and no mention of another child. Anyway, they already had the first one and that hadn't stopped her.'

'Perhaps she did something that put her in a position where she had to resign.'

'Like what?'

'Goodness, I don't know,' said Watson. 'That's like asking me why the chicken crossed the road. There are so many possibilities.'

'Hmm,' was Slater's only response.

Watson observed him over her coffee cup. 'Do you think it's important? Because it's obviously worrying you.'

'I have no idea,' said Slater, 'but my gut tells me something's not right, and Norm always says you should never ignore your gut. Although in his case, it would be difficult to ignore.'

Watson smiled at the reference. Norm, or Norman Norman, to give him his full name, was Slater's friend and former colleague. A rather rotund individual, he had recently suffered a heart attack and was now having to face up to the fact he needed to change his lifestyle — or else. 'How's he getting on?' she asked.

'Last time I saw him he was twenty pounds lighter than when he keeled over and making good progress.'

'D'you think he'll stick to it?'

'I hope so,' said Slater. 'I really hope so.' He stared into the distance for a moment. 'Anyway, back to Diana Randall.

I think we need to take a closer look at her, even if it's just to satisfy my own curiosity.'

'I'll get onto it when we get back,' said Watson.

'No, it's okay. I think I should do it. I want you to see if you can learn any more about this pendant.'

CHAPTER TEN

As they pulled up back at their mobile office, a visibly excited Henry Cutter appeared. 'Have you two had a chance to check your email today?'

'We've been out all day,' said Slater. 'We haven't really had time.'

'They've finished the DNA analysis, and when they ran it against the database, they got a hit!'

'How did that happen? Did the parents submit a sample when the boy went missing?' asked Watson.

'I don't know about that,' said Cutter. 'All I know is the father is called David Hudson.'

'Hudson?' repeated Slater in surprise.

'According to the experts, David Hudson is the father. They didn't find a match for the mother. Her DNA's not on the database.'

'So it's not Alan and Diana Randall?' asked Slater, his voice filled with disappointment.

'I'm afraid not.'

Slater puffed out his cheeks. 'Well, I won't deny I'm surprised.'

'Sorry,' said Cutter, 'but DNA doesn't lie.'

'So who's this Hudson guy? And what's he done to get himself on the database.'

'They didn't send that much detail,' said Cutter. 'You'll have to find that out for yourself.'

Slater turned to Watson, but she was already on her way up the steps to their office door. 'I'm on it,' she said, unlocking the door and disappearing inside.

'You look a bit miffed,' said Cutter to Slater.

'Well, yeah, I have to admit I am a bit disappointed in a way. I was convinced we'd found Sonny Randall, and I was even beginning to think his parents might have killed him.'

'So I guess I've spoilt your day again,' said Cutter. 'I'm sorry about that.' He was silent for a moment. 'Of course, it's possible David Hudson knew Mrs Randall, and they were more than just friends.'

Slater looked doubtful. 'I suppose it would explain a few things.'

'Then again, maybe I just like the idea of starting a malicious rumour,' admitted Cutter with a rueful grin.

Slater smiled. 'There's definitely something funny about that woman. I swear she recognised the pendant, but she was adamant it couldn't be her son.'

'Did you get a DNA sample from them?'

'They point-blank refused,' said Slater, 'and then her husband threw us out.'

'So maybe I'm right and they know it's not his kid,' said Cutter.

'Yeah, but what's the point? We're going to find out anyway.'

'That maybe so, but that doesn't mean he's going to help you do it. If I'm right, you're just about to ruin their lives. Why would he want to help you do that?'

Slater could see Cutter's point. 'I'll bear your malicious rumour theory in mind,' he said as he headed for his office. 'I've heard crazier ideas.'

* * *

'So, what do we know?' asked Slater as he walked into the office.

Watson didn't look up from her laptop. 'Well, we know it looks like Diana Randall was right. It can't be her son, can it?'

'Henry thinks maybe she knew Hudson.'

'What do you think?'

Slater pulled a face. 'We can't afford to rule it out, at least not yet. And you have to admit, it might explain her weird behaviour.'

'I can't argue with that,' agreed Watson. 'But whoever the father is, I still think I was right, and that was just her way of dealing with it.'

'Hmm, maybe,' conceded Slater, moodily. 'Anyway, what do we have on this Hudson bloke?'

'I'm just getting to it,' said Watson, studying her screen. 'Ah, here we are. David Hudson, sentenced to six months in prison for assaulting a police officer.'

'When was this?'

'It says here he was sentenced in March 2001,' said Watson. 'It was local, too. The assault took place in Ramlinstoke Police Station.'

'Does it say who he thumped, and why?'

'It says the lead officer was a DS Colin Norton.'

'That begs the question: what was Hudson doing in Ramlinstoke Police Station?' asked Slater. 'I think it's a bit of a coincidence that he should smack a copper on the nose less than five miles from where his son was found.'

'But it was years before he died,' said Watson. 'Do you think it could be relevant?'

'I'm beginning to wonder if anything we've learnt so far is relevant,' said Slater, absently. He was scanning through the list of missing children they had been sent. 'But there is something worrying me that definitely is relevant.'

'What's that?' asked Watson.

Slater looked up from his list. 'If this is Hudson's son we've found, then why isn't he on this missing kids list?'

CHAPTER ELEVEN

Slater was immersed in scouring records to find out whatever he could about Diana Randall. He had tasked Watson to do the same for David Hudson. Unlikely as it might seem, it was always possible they could find a connection that proved they knew each other and that Cutter's malicious rumour was actually correct.

As Slater had thought, Diana Randall had indeed been a bit special. She hadn't just been a high-flyer, she had been positively stratospheric. So much so that she had made the move to Flipton to become DI at just thirty years of age, and yet, just four years later, she had resigned. He could find nothing to suggest exactly why she had resigned, which was suspicious in itself as far as he was concerned. He wondered if Superintendent Bradshaw might be able to help find out why. He'd known all about Slater's past, after all, so it was worth asking. He rattled off a quick email to his boss and went back to his research.

Now that was interesting. Diana Randall had been a DS at Ramlinstoke before she transferred to Flipton. That would have been, what, eighteen years ago? And hadn't Watson said Hudson had been in Ramlinstoke around that time? The plot was definitely thickening.

'Get this,' he said to Watson, who looked up from the computer screen. 'Diana Randall was a DS, here in Ramlinstoke, before she got the DI job at Flipton.'

'But she never mentioned that when we told her where the body had been found!'

'So, you spotted that, too? It makes you wonder why she would keep that to herself, doesn't it?'

'Her husband kept quiet about it, too,' Watson pointed out.

'Yeah,' said Slater. 'Whatever's going on, he's part of it.'

Diana had married Alan Randall when she was twenty-six. He was fourteen years her senior. Slater wasted a couple of minutes on idle speculation about what the attraction was, and then remembered the house and what Watson had told him about how Randall made a living. There was obviously plenty of money sloshing around, and Slater very much doubted it was Diana's.

He continued going back into her history. Her maiden name was Murphy. Hadn't the pendant been made by an Irish silversmith? He wondered if that proved anything. He thought probably not, but it wouldn't hurt to pass the information back to the team at base. They were looking into the pendant so it wouldn't hurt to see if there was a connection.

He decided he'd wait to see if Bradshaw could come up with anything relating to Diana's resignation and logged out of the database. Then he turned his attention to the file they had picked up from Flipton. He was hoping there would perhaps be something in there that would give him a lead, but it didn't take long for him to realise this had been a pretty thorough, and intensive, investigation. No stone seemed to have been left unturned in their search for young Sonny Randall, and yet for all that effort, they had no idea what had happened or where he had gone. Slater knew from experience just how intensive a missing child investigation could be. It hardly seemed possible that so much effort could have failed to produce a result, yet that's what appeared to have happened.

As he reached the last page of the file, he felt slightly guilty at the idea he should be checking up on his colleagues at Flipton when he knew they must have gone through all this information again and again hoping to find something they had missed.

'Well, if it's there, I've missed it too,' he muttered.

'Sorry, sir, did you speak?' asked Watson, from her side of the tiny office.

'Just mumbling to myself.' Slater closed the file, leaned back in his chair, yawned extravagantly, and stretched his back. Then he got up to stretch his legs. 'Well, apart from the fact Diana Randall worked in Ramlinstoke before she moved to Flipton, I'm afraid I've come up with nothing significant, so I hope you're doing better,' he said. 'Have you found an address for David Hudson?'

Watson tapped away at her keyboard and studied her screen. 'David Hudson, born August 1976, both parents died when he was young, spent most of his childhood in care, joined the army at eighteen, left four years later. There doesn't seem to be a current address. His last known address is from ten years ago. But I think you'll find it quite interesting.' She turned to Slater. 'He was living in Flipton Dene.'

'This is all very coincidental, isn't it?' said Slater. 'And it's not exactly a big village. There must be a chance he might have known the Randalls.'

'A very good chance, I would think,' said Watson, studying her screen again. 'I've just pulled it up on the map. He lived in a cottage on a farm owned by a Major Stanley. Guess who one of the major's neighbours is?'

'You're kidding,' said Slater.

'Remember that lane the Randalls' house is on? Well, Major Stanley's farm is at the end of it. He would have driven past their house every time he came out to go anywhere.'

'So we know Hudson is the father of the dead child, and we suspect Diana Randall is the mother. We also know he left there ten years ago, and that the Randalls' little boy also disappeared ten years ago,' said Slater.

'Surely they would have checked that out at the time,' said Watson.

'I would hope so,' agreed Slater, 'but they didn't know he was the child's father, did they? There's certainly no mention of it in their case file. As far as I'm concerned, he becomes much more significant now we know that.'

'But are we sure there really is a connection between the two cases?'

'No,' said Slater. 'But we're not sure there isn't one, and as we know for sure Hudson is the father of our victim, we need to find him, and find out what we can about him. See if you can find a phone number for this Major Stanley. Give him a call and see if he's willing to tell us anything about Hudson. I'm going to see if I can speak to this DS Norton that Hudson assaulted. Maybe he can give us some insight into the man. Then I'll make the tea.'

Five minutes later, Slater carried two mugs of steaming tea into the office. Watson looked up as he approached. 'The major says Hudson moved on ten years ago, but if we would like to pay him a visit, he would be more than happy to talk to us. He says he can tell us quite a lot about Hudson. Apparently he served under the major in the army.'

'Oh, great,' said Slater. 'Make us an appointment for—'

'We're seeing him tomorrow morning,' said Watson. 'I hope that's okay?'

Slater smiled. 'Good work, Watson.'

'Any luck with DS Norton?'

'It'll have to keep,' said Slater. 'Apparently he's away on leave. Not back until next week.'

CHAPTER TWELVE

As they drove up the lane to reach the major's farm, Slater couldn't stop himself from staring at the Randalls' house.

'You'd really like to have another go at them, wouldn't you?' asked Watson.

'It would be fair to say they're somewhere near the top of my wish list,' he agreed. 'I'm sure we have unfinished business with the Randalls, it's just that, right now, I'm not quite sure what it is.'

For some reason he couldn't explain, Slater had a picture in his head of what the major was going to look like. In Slater's mind, he was going to be a short, plump, ruddy-faced man in his seventies, who would be full of bluster and endlessly complaining about the youth of today. In fact, Major Stanley was nothing like that, being very slim, upright, and six feet two inches tall. His handsome, fifty-something face was topped with a head of thick fair hair, and his bright blue eyes had a sharpness about them that told them he was no fool.

'This farmhouse has been in the family for generations,' he explained as he led them into the house. 'It doesn't look much from the outside, but we've made a lot of improvements inside.' He opened a door and stepped back to allow them through.

'Goodness!' said Watson as she walked into the room. 'Now this is what I call a kitchen. I could fit my whole flat in here.'

'It's taken a lot of work to bring it all up to date,' said the major, proudly. 'My wife is the one with the vision, I just keep the farm going to pay for it all.'

'This is very nice,' said Slater. 'I wouldn't mind a kitchen like this myself.'

'Well, thank you,' said the major. He fussed around making coffee for everyone while they continued to talk about the farm. 'This small talk is all very well,' he said as he carried a tray with their drinks across to the table, 'but I know you didn't come here to admire my wife's flair for kitchen design. Why don't you sit down and we can get down to business? You don't mind sitting at the kitchen table, do you?'

'Not at all,' said Slater. 'It's much more practical for taking notes than balancing a notebook on a knee.'

'Are you allowed to tell me why you want to know about David?' asked the major.

'I can tell you his name has come up in an investigation. We're not sure exactly how he fits in at the moment, and as we're not sure where he is, we can't actually speak to him directly. We're hoping you can give us some background and maybe a clue as to where he might be.'

'Keeping it vague, eh, Inspector? Can't say I expected much else really. So, what do you want to know?'

'I suppose the first question I have to ask is how did David Hudson come to be living in one of your cottages?' asked Slater.

'Let me start at the beginning,' said the major. 'I first met David Hudson when he was a young private in the army. He would have been about eighteen years old. He was a quiet, shy lad, but like any eighteen-year-old, he liked to go out with his mates and have a drink. The problem for Hudson was his height and size. He was still a boy, but in a man's body. At six feet five inches, and seventeen stone, he literally stood out from the crowd, and that made him a target.

45

'You know what it's like, squaddies are often targeted by local thugs, and the bigger the squaddie, the more people want to take him on. Consequently, he got into a fight nearly every weekend, and every Monday morning he would be wheeled into my office on a charge.'

'He didn't start the fights then?' asked Slater.

'Good heavens, no! He was a real gentle giant. Most times he didn't even retaliate when he *did* get picked on.'

'Not being prepared to fight back hardly sounds like the make-up of a soldier,' Slater observed.

'Actually, the ones who see red don't make very good soldiers,' said the major. 'You want cool heads, not short fuses, but that's getting off the point. David Hudson was a bright young man who showed a lot of promise, but because he was such a frequent Monday-morning visitor, I knew he wasn't going to get very far unless someone showed a bit of interest in his future.'

'So you started to look out for him?' asked Watson.

'I tried to do it for all my men, especially the younger ones. It's all very well having corporals and sergeants shouting at you all the time, but sometimes these young lads need a father figure. Hudson probably needed that more than most as he was an orphan.'

'So you got to know him?' Slater asked.

Major Stanley gave a little smile. 'It's a delicate balancing act. You know someone needs a bit of help and encouragement, but you can't be seen to be showing favour towards anyone.'

'But you managed?'

'I think I was probably the first person who had taken an interest in him. He was interested in machines, and in farming, so with my farming background it was quite easy for me to encourage that interest. I persuaded him that if he wanted to get into farming when he left the army, he needed to study.'

'And did he?'

'I'll say! He didn't exactly become a bookworm, but he cut back on the drinking and socialising and focused on his studies. For the first time, he knew what he wanted to do with the rest of his life.'

'So you saved him from himself?' suggested Watson.

'No, I don't think that's fair,' said the major. 'That makes it sound like he was a big problem, but that's not how it was. I didn't save him from anything, he did it all himself. I showed him the way, but then he saved himself — not from himself, but from his circumstances.'

'It sounds as if you had a lot of time for him,' said Slater.

'I have lots of time for anyone who can recognise they're going nowhere and do something about it, Inspector. So should we all.'

Slater thought that was fair comment, even if it had been delivered like a reprimand. 'What happened next?'

'What happens to all of us? He met a girl and fell in love. Her name was Kylie Mason.'

'How old would he have been then?'

'About twenty, I think.'

'Did it last?' asked Watson.

'Oh yes, it was the real thing, believe me. You could see it in his eyes. Now he had even more purpose about him. About a year later he told me he would be leaving the army to get married and work on a farm. As far as he was concerned, he had found his happy ending. And when he left, I really didn't expect to see him again.'

'So how did he come to end up in prison for assaulting a police officer?' asked Slater. 'That wasn't very gentle, was it? Didn't you feel let down?'

'I couldn't believe it when I heard he was in prison,' admitted the major. 'And yes, at first I was very disappointed, but I knew there had to be more to it. I couldn't accept he would have punched a policeman without a damned good reason. So I went to see him.'

'That was beyond the call of duty, wasn't it?' asked Slater. 'I mean, he'd already left the army.'

The major gave Slater a pitiful look. 'It wasn't beyond my duty as a human being.'

Slater felt slightly irritated at this second ticking off from the major in as many minutes, but this was all good background and he didn't want to spoil it. 'Err, yes, quite right,' he said. 'So why did Hudson punch a police officer?'

'Before he left the army, he had one more tour of duty to do. It was six months trying to keep the peace in Kosovo. By this time, Kylie was pregnant, but before he left the country he had found them somewhere to live. Kylie was going to move into the cottage in October while he was away, and he would be home a couple of weeks before Christmas. They had their whole lives planned out.'

'But?' asked Slater.

'When he got back home, Kylie should have had the baby and been in their cottage for a couple of months. I remember he got a letter telling him he was a father while we were only halfway through the tour. Of course, we have the internet and email these days, but back then, the best way to communicate was still by letter, so if anything had gone wrong after that, he would have had no way of knowing unless she had written to tell him.'

'So what *had* gone wrong?'

'When he got to what he thought was his new home, there was no sign of Kylie. What's more, the people living there told him they had never heard of a Kylie! According to their story, they had moved into the cottage in the middle of November and the place was empty before that.'

'So, where was Kylie?' asked Watson.

'That's the million-dollar question,' said the major, 'and as far as I'm aware, we still don't know the answer. Of course David went straight to the police and reported his family missing, but he told me he felt they never took him seriously.'

'What made him say that?' asked Slater.

'Because there was no sign of Kylie or their possessions at the cottage, the police at first seemed to assume David was making the whole thing up. Then, when he persisted, they told him that even if his story was true, Kylie was an adult and as such, had the right to go wherever she wanted without having to tell anyone.'

'Why didn't he come to you?' asked Watson.

'The poor lad thought he couldn't as he was no longer in the army. It's a pity because there was so much I could have done to help him, but he was so far out of his depth I don't think he could put two thoughts together. And then, when he was out of his mind with worry, one of the police officers told him Kylie had been taking him for a ride all long. He said she had probably planned to run off with someone else all along, and that's why there was no sign of their stuff in the cottage.'

'And that's when he punched the man's lights out,' finished Slater.

'He did six months in prison,' said the major, 'and then I managed to get him released on parole. The conditions were that he had to live on the farm here, in one of the cottages, and work for me. He was still a prisoner, in effect, but I hoped if I could get him out of prison and keep him out, I could help him rebuild his life.'

'You thought he had been unfairly treated and deserved a second chance,' said Slater.

'Exactly! I'm not condoning what he did, but can you imagine coming home for Christmas thinking you're going to spend the rest of your life with your family and then finding them gone? I've met that DS Norton. My goodness, if there was a prize for being obnoxious, that horrible little man would win it every time.'

'Norton?' asked Slater. 'DS Colin Norton from Ramlinstoke?'

'Yes, that's the man.'

'Do you mind if I ask how you met him?' asked Watson. 'Was it over David Hudson's case?'

'No, it was years later. I suppose it's a bit unfair to condemn him as a bad man. He can't be all bad. I met him when the Randalls' son disappeared. They're neighbours just down the lane there. He came to support the family and volunteered for all the searches.'

Slater was getting that old familiar tingly feeling. He glanced at Watson. She had perked up too. 'Did he know them?' asked Slater.

'Apparently he had worked with Diana before, had become a family friend, and kept in touch.'

'Would David Hudson have known Diana Randall?' asked Slater.

'Yes, of course. The Randalls were good friends of ours and often came over. David was always treated as one of the family so he would often be here too.' The major made a big deal of looking at his watch. 'I really have to be getting on.'

'Yes, thank you, Major, you've been very helpful,' said Slater. 'There is one more thing. Do you know where David Hudson is now?'

'I have an address, but I doubt it will be much use. He moved on ten years ago. I wrote to him two or three times, but I never got a reply. I had the feeling he'd left here to get away from all of us.' He found an address book, opened it, and gave it to Watson. 'It's the top one there.'

Watson copied the address into her notebook.

'Can you tell me what this is about?' asked the major as they got ready to leave.

'We've found a child's body,' said Slater. 'DNA testing indicates David Hudson was the father. We'd like to find him so we can tell him.'

The major took a sharp intake of breath. 'Oh my God,' he said, shaking his head. 'You will be careful, won't you? I did my best to help him rebuild his life, but he remains heartbroken. It's a very deep wound you're going to reopen.'

CHAPTER THIRTEEN

Slater had elected to drive back from the major's to allow Watson to call the team back at base. He had tuned her telephone conversations out almost straight away and had been deep in thought ever since they had left Flipton Dene. Last night, for the third night running, he'd had yet another heated exchange with Jenny, and he was beginning to wonder what was behind it all. He didn't feel he was being unreasonable in not wanting to drive for hours every day. It wouldn't be forever, after all.

Once he got settled in his new base, the plan was to find a house and then they could be together every night. They had agreed all this weeks ago, and yet now she seemed to have forgotten and did nothing but complain. He was beginning to wonder if maybe this was a warning of things to come, and if he was honest, he was beginning to have second thoughts about the whole relationship. He became vaguely aware someone was talking to him.

'Hello? Hello? Is there anybody in there?' called Watson.

'I'm so sorry,' he said. 'I was miles away.'

'I wasn't sure if you were deep in thought or in some sort of trance,' said Watson.

'I was trying to make sense of it all,' said Slater. 'I'm sorry. What were you saying?'

'Okay, the wheels are turning. Now we have a location and a rough idea when this Kylie Mason and her son went missing, I've got the team searching for the missing persons report Hudson says he made. I've also given them the address Hudson gave to the major and made it a priority to find him. I'm afraid it means the pendant gets put on the back burner for now, but I'm sure you agree finding David Hudson is our main priority now.'

'Definitely,' said Slater. 'You realise there could be another reason for his broken heart?'

'You mean they might have disappeared because he killed them himself?' asked Watson. 'Yes, I thought that was a possibility, too, but if he was telling the truth about the cottage, and Kylie moved in during October, he couldn't have done it. He was in Kosovo.'

'Yes,' agreed Slater, 'but the major said the people in the cottage said it was empty when they moved in. What if he made that up, and Kylie was already dead before he went to Kosovo?' He felt pleased with himself, but his pleasure was short-lived as Watson immediately shot his theory down in flames.

'Sorry, boss, but I'm not sure that works,' she said, nervously.

'Why not?'

'Don't forget she had the baby while he was away. If he had murdered her before he went, she would still have been carrying. He wouldn't have got the letter telling him he was a daddy.'

'He could have sent it himself,' countered Slater, then he thought about it for a moment. 'Nah. You're right, it's a non-runner, isn't it? That would mean a lot of advanced planning, and from what the major was saying this guy doesn't sound like a criminal mastermind, does he?' He glanced across and gave her a reassuring smile. 'Good work.'

'I'm sorry,' she said. 'I know it's not my place to tell you what I think, but—'

'Oh, but it is!' he assured her. 'I told you before, we're a team. It's no good having a brain as good as yours on the case if you're not going to contribute anything. You need to get it into your head that I don't want a "yes sir, no sir" robot alongside me, I want someone with an opinion who's not afraid to voice it. I'm just as capable of going off in the wrong direction as anyone else, and if you think that's what I'm doing, I want you to tell me. It could save both of us a lot of embarrassment, especially me.'

'Oh, I see,' said Watson. 'Right, I'll try to remember that in future.' Her mobile phone began to ring, and she snatched it up and listened to the voice on the other end. 'Apparently no missing person report was ever made by David Hudson about Kylie Mason and her son,' she told Slater as she ended the call.

'But that makes no sense. He must have approached Ramlinstoke station about something,' said Slater. 'He was actually in there when he belted Norton.'

'Do you believe this story about her going missing?' asked Watson.

'Well, I'm beginning to lean that way,' said Slater. 'You've just proved he couldn't have killed them before he went away because of the baby, and the major certainly seemed to think it was kosher, and I got the impression he's no fool. Even so, I think I'll feel happier if we can actually find Hudson and speak to him ourselves.'

They drove on in silence for a couple of minutes before Slater spoke again. 'So, we know we need to find Hudson, but where do we go in the meantime? What's our next step in this investigation?'

Watson thumbed through the notebook on her lap. 'What about trying to find a connection between Hudson and Diana Randall?'

'So you noticed the major was suddenly in a hurry for us to leave when I asked about that?'

'It could have been that he really was in a hurry,' suggested Watson.

'You're too forgiving,' said Slater with a wry smile. 'Let's get it checked out anyway. Let's make sure we leave no stone unturned and all that.'

Watson made a note in her notebook.

'Anything else?' asked Slater.

'DS Norton seems to be cropping up rather a lot,' said Watson. 'I really think we need to speak to him.'

'Yes, I have a feeling I'm going to enjoy that particular conversation,' said Slater.

* * *

They were just fifteen minutes away from Trillington village when Watson's phone rang again. There was a brief conversation, during which she glanced several times in Slater's direction. Finally, she ended the call. 'I'm sure the boss will be delighted to provide a bottle for your birthday.'

'Does Bradshaw know you spend his money like that?' asked Slater as she ended the call and put the phone back in her lap.

'Do you mean about the bottle?' she asked.

'Yeah.'

'Oh, I didn't mean him,' she said with a broad grin. 'Didn't you say we should call you the boss?'

'But I don't even know who you were talking to!' Slater protested.

'Her name is Shanaya, and she's a very bright, talented and beautiful young lady who works in our offices back at base. She's one of the best we've got, and the reason you're providing the bubbly is because she has found David Hudson.'

Slater was suitably impressed. 'That was damned quick. How did she manage that?'

'While the rest of us were assuming he had gone into hiding, like some sort of outlaw, Shanaya considered an alternative idea. It occurred to her that maybe he wasn't hiding at all but was perhaps living abroad, and if he wasn't hiding, it was quite likely he would still be using his real name.'

Slater couldn't help but smile at the simplicity of it. 'So she did a search and . . . ?'

'He's living in France. He manages a small farm with a campsite and a few gîtes. She's going to email us the address and any other info she can find. It should be waiting for us at the office.'

'D'you know, I thought it would take us ages to find him,' confessed Slater. 'You're right, the boss will be delighted to provide a bottle for Shanaya's birthday. In fact, I might even buy her a whole case!'

'I'd better book us tickets to France,' said Watson. 'When would you like to go?'

'Sooner rather than later, I think,' said Slater.

'I've never used the Eurotunnel before, it'll be a bit of an adventure,' said Watson, sounding like a kid with a new toy.

Slater glanced across at her. She did actually look excited, but he didn't share her delight. 'Ah, yes, about that,' he said. 'I'm not a big fan of tunnels. I even get a bit queasy driving under a motorway bridge.'

Watson looked at him, mouth open in disbelief. 'Really?'

'I'm afraid so, ever since I can remember.'

'Well, fancy that!' She looked away but Slater detected the hint of a smile on her face.

'I suppose you think I'm weird?'

'The word I would use is "different",' she said. 'I'd definitely say you were different. Anyway, it doesn't matter, we can take the ferry. I love standing on deck watching the water go by.'

'I'm afraid I'm not mad about boats either,' he said, with a half-smile.

'Oh dear, that's going to make life difficult.'

'A ferry is big enough to be okay,' he said. 'It's little boats I hate. A ferry will be fine, as long as I don't have to look over the side. You'll have to do that on your own. I'll stay in the bar.'

CHAPTER FOURTEEN

After a thankfully calm crossing, Slater and Watson disembarked the ferry and Slater tentatively pulled out onto the open road. While he drove, Watson described the farm from the information they had downloaded. Set in a valley, surrounded by farmland, there were ten gites on the farm — some created from converted barns and some purpose-built log cabins. The original farmhouse housed the reception area and also served as a small shop selling a few essentials and produce from farms in the local area.

'It looks as good as it sounds,' she remarked as Slater turned the car off the road. 'Just the sort of place to come if you wanted to have a quiet break and do some walking.'

'If you're that keen, you can make a booking while we're here,' said Slater. 'But perhaps you should curb your enthusiasm until after we've spoken to the suspect.'

Watson looked like she had a retort on the tip of her tongue, but Slater gave her a look.

'Is that how we're going to treat him?' she asked.

'That's what he is,' said Slater as he parked the car, 'but we'll stick to the plan and approach him as the father and see where it goes from there.'

They climbed from the car and made their way through the door marked *Reception*. As Watson pushed the door open, they heard a bell ring somewhere deeper in the house. Almost straight away, a curtain behind the counter was swished back and a big, tall man ducked his way through to greet them. He had large, rugged hands and the sort of deep suntan that came from working out in the fields. The lifestyle obviously suited him, and he didn't appear to have changed much from the photograph the major had given them.

'*Bonjour*,' he said, with a big amiable smile.

'Bonjour,' said Slater and Watson in unison.

The man's smile widened. 'Ah! You're English.'

'My accent never was much use,' admitted Slater.

'How can I help you?'

'David Hudson?' said Slater.

'That's me,' he said, cheerfully.

Slater flashed his warrant card. 'I'm DI Slater, and this is DS Brearley. D'you think we could have a word?'

'What's it about?'

'It might be better if there was somewhere a bit more private where we could talk,' Slater suggested quietly.

Hudson's expression had changed from amused curiosity to confused concern. 'Now you're worrying me. I've just spoken to my wife, so I know she's in town and she's okay, and I don't have any other family so it can't be anything like that.'

'Don't you have a son?' asked Slater.

The colour seemed to drain from Hudson's face, and his mouth flapped open once or twice before he managed to squeeze any words out. 'Jesus! That was another lifetime ago.'

'I'm sorry,' said Slater. 'I can see this has come as a bit of a shock. Are you sure we can't sit down somewhere?'

'Err, yes, come on through.' Like a man in a daze, he led them through a door into the kitchen. He pointed to a rather rustic-looking table. 'Take a seat,' he said. They took adjoining seats, and Hudson chose to sit opposite them.

'I don't understand,' he said as he slumped into his chair. 'There must be some sort of mistake. I know I fathered a son once, but that was years ago. I've never actually set eyes on him.'

'I know this must be very confusing for you,' said Slater. 'The thing is, we've uncovered a little boy's body, and DNA evidence tells us you're his father.'

Hudson stared at Slater for a moment and then buried his face in his hands.

'I'll make us some tea,' said Watson, getting up from the table.

'Where did you find him?' asked Hudson eventually. 'And his mother? Was she with him?'

'I'm afraid we found him buried just outside a village called Trillington,' explained Slater, careful to avoid mention of the ditch he was actually found in. 'He was alone.'

'I always knew something like this must have happened,' Hudson said. 'I told the police at the time, but they wouldn't listen to me. They told me I was making it up, that she'd run off with another man, but I knew that couldn't be right.'

'If you're talking about your girlfriend, we haven't found her,' said Slater.

'She wouldn't have left the baby,' said Hudson. 'She just wouldn't.'

Watson appeared with three cups of tea.

'The child we found wasn't a baby,' said Slater. 'We're not sure of his exact age yet, but we believe he was between six and ten years old. He had been dead for about ten years when we found him.'

Now Hudson added confusion to his distressed face.

'That can't be right,' he said. 'I searched that village. They weren't there, either of them. If they had run away, why would they have come back? It makes no sense.'

'Do you know a woman called Diana Randall?' asked Slater.

'Yes, I know her. I used to work and live on a farm owned by a man called Major Stanley. Diana was one of his neighbours.'

'How would you describe your relationship with her?'

A puzzled frown creased Hudson's forehead. 'I didn't have a relationship with her. She was just a friend of a friend.'

'But you socialised with her?'

'The major and his wife were very good to me. They treated me like one of the family. If he was having friends round, he would often invite me to join them so, yes, I would have had a drink with her and her husband on occasions. Why are you asking me about her? What has she got to do with anything?'

'You know she lost a son?'

'Yes, I did know. He disappeared a couple of weeks before I moved away. I did help with the first searches, but I'd taken this job here and they needed me so I had to leave.'

Slater produced some photos and set them down on the table. 'These are one or two items found with the body that made us think the child we found was Diana Randall's son, but she says it's not. Do you recognise any of them?'

'But you just said he was *my* son,' said Hudson. He frowned as he glanced at the photos. He was obviously confused. Then the frown suddenly vanished as he realised what Slater was suggesting. 'What? You think I'm the father of her son?' he asked indignantly. 'That boy was born before I moved up there. I didn't even know Diana Randall back then.'

'I'm sorry, but I had to ask the question,' said Slater, beginning to wish he had handled this some other way.

'Why don't you tell us what happened back then, Mr Hudson?' Watson suggested quickly.

Hudson got up from his chair and walked across to a sideboard, slid a drawer open, and removed an old biscuit tin. He removed the lid as he walked back to the table and sat down again. He passed a couple of photos across to them.

'Here she is,' he said. 'This is the only woman I've ever had a baby with. Her name was Kylie Mason.'

Slater and Watson looked at the photos. A pretty face surrounded by wild, blonde curls smiled back at them. She was obviously still in her teens.

'That was when we first met,' explained Hudson. 'She was sixteen, and I was twenty, but I was still a kid really. I was in the army. Major Stanley had sort of taken me under his wing, and for the first time I had a bit of confidence. I'd never had the courage to ask a girl out before, and I was sure she'd turn me down, but she said yes! It didn't take long before I knew she was the one for me, but her parents hated me. They tried everything to keep us apart. When I told them we wanted to get married, that was the last straw. They kicked Kylie out.

'She got a little flat, but I had to help her out with the rent, and of course we spent a lot of time there, just the two of us, and it seemed sort of perfect somehow. So I decided I should leave the army. If her parents weren't going to look after her, I thought it should be me. Then we found out she was pregnant and there was no way we could have raised a kid in that tiny flat so we looked around for somewhere a bit bigger.

'We found a little cottage on the outskirts of that village, Trillington, and we were all set to move in. Kylie was going to move in towards the end of October, and two months later, after I finished my last tour, I was going to join her. I even spoke to a farmer nearby about the possibility of a job when I got out.'

He fished around in the tin and produced some more photos. This time, Kylie was in various stages of her pregnancy. Then another two of a tiny baby. 'These were the last photos she sent me. I was away on that final tour.' He took a long, lingering look at the photos before passing them over. 'Fancy being away when your baby is born. I should have been there,' he said, sadly.

'That's a very sweet-looking baby,' said Watson.

'He took after his mother,' said Hudson, proudly.

'So what happened when you came back?' asked Slater.

'I got back two weeks before Christmas, bags full of presents for my family, only when I got to what I thought was my home, there was no sign of them. The people living there said they'd never heard of anyone called Kylie. They claimed they had moved in in the middle of November and the place had been empty before that.'

'You'd not heard from Kylie?' asked Slater.

'We didn't have access to the internet back then,' explained Hudson. 'We couldn't afford a telephone in Kylie's flat, or at the cottage, so we had to rely on letters. I admit I was worried when the letters stopped, but what could I do?' He fumbled through the tin again until he found a folded letter. 'Here's the last one she sent me. It was a couple of days before she was due to move into the cottage. She was a good mother — it says in the letter how the baby's not a good sleeper, but he would fall asleep if she walked around with him. Kylie had taken to wearing one of those baby sling things so she could carry the baby in front of her. She'd go out walking late at night to get him off to sleep.'

Slater unfolded the letter, read through it, and passed it on to Watson.

'Like I said, I was worried when she didn't write again,' said Hudson, 'but she had a little baby to deal with, and a new cottage to worry about, and I was going to be there in a few weeks anyway . . .' He came to a choking halt, and Slater gave him a minute or two to compose himself.

'I assume you went to the police?'

'They told me they thought I was making it up, or that she'd just run off,' said Hudson. 'They asked me how come there was no trace of them anywhere?'

'How did you explain that?' asked Slater.

'I couldn't,' admitted Hudson, 'but I just knew my Kylie wouldn't do that to me. We had no secrets; she would have told me. I even showed that letter to the police, but he just ignored it.'

'When you say "the police", who exactly are you referring to?'

'Detective Sergeant Norton,' said Hudson. 'You must know that. I'm sure you know I have a criminal record.'

'Assault, wasn't it?' asked Slater. 'What happened?'

'I was getting frustrated that he wouldn't listen to me,' said Hudson, 'and then, one day, he said he thought she had been leading me on all the time. He said I was just a sucker and that it probably wasn't my baby at all. That's when I punched his lights out.'

'Do you have a short temper?' asked Slater.

'I don't think so. It took me two weeks of being ignored, humiliated and fobbed off to get to that stage, and even then I only hit him once.'

Slater looked at the size of Hudson's hands, and thought one punch would probably be more than sufficient to flatten most opponents.

'I have to tell you, we've been unable to find a missing persons report made out at that time for Kylie and your son,' said Slater.

'Are you trying to tell me you think I'm making this up, too?' asked Hudson. 'Why don't you look up my court case? It'll tell you in there what my excuse was for punching him. The magistrate seemed to think it was a pretty good reason. And what other reason would I have for leaving the army and heading for that village in the middle of nowhere? Why would I have spent the previous two weeks making daily visits to that police station? You must have spoken to the major. What did he say?'

'He says it's a pity you didn't go to him for help.'

'I'd just left the army, I didn't think I could go straight back begging for help. I was supposed to be standing on my own two feet.'

'Why did you give the major a false address when you moved out?' asked Slater.

Hudson sighed and gave them a rueful smile. 'The major and his wife are wonderful people,' he said, 'and what they did for me probably saved my life, but at the same time they were a permanent reminder of my past. I came here because I wanted to get away from everything to do with my past, turn over a new leaf, and start again. I've often thought I could have handled it better, but when the Randalls' son disappeared we were all under suspicion, and then out of nowhere DS Norton turned up on the scene. I didn't trust him not to start accusing me, so I decided covering my tracks might be a smart move.'

'What makes you think you're not still a suspect?' asked Slater.

'If you want to arrest me, can you wait until my wife comes home? I wouldn't want her worrying where I was. But was I difficult to find? No, because I've done nothing wrong, and I'm not hiding.'

'Did you contact Kylie's parents and tell them what had happened?' asked Watson.

'I tried,' said Hudson. 'But they wouldn't speak to me, except to say running away from me was probably the best thing she could have done.'

'Do you think she went back to them?'

'I didn't know what to think back then,' said Hudson, 'but I've always believed she would have been there waiting for me unless something terrible had happened to her.'

'Do you have an address for her parents?' asked Slater. 'I'd quite like to talk to them.'

'I've got the address where they lived back then,' said Hudson, fumbling through the tin once again, 'but I have no idea if they're still there. They might be dead for all I know.' He handed Watson a slip of paper.

Watson wrote the address in her notebook and offered it back to Hudson. 'No, you can keep it. I shan't need it again,' he said.

Slater didn't really think they were going to get much more out of Hudson. Now was probably a good time to leave.

'Look, Inspector,' said Hudson, 'I'm not stupid. I know you probably think I'm involved in this affair in some way, but I can promise you I haven't been near Trillington village since I came out of prison. I hardly ever went out when I was living at the major's, and I haven't been back to England once since I moved here.'

'I won't pretend you're wrong,' Slater said. 'In cases like this, everyone tends to be a suspect until we can eliminate them. We'll check what you've told us and see where we are after that.'

'So you're not going to take me back with you?'

'I don't think that will be necessary,' Slater said. 'I don't think you're going to run away.'

'What's going to happen to my son? I think I'd like to arrange the funeral.'

Slater smiled sadly. 'I don't think the body will be released just yet. We'll have to let you know.'

CHAPTER FIFTEEN

Slater had been driving in silence for the fifteen minutes since they had left David Hudson. He was hunched over the steering wheel, totally focused on the road. Watson had been quiet since they had left; he appreciated her knack of knowing when he wanted to be left to his thoughts.

At last, he let out a sigh and sat back in his seat. 'So now we know why Hudson's son didn't appear on that list of missing kids. The poor devil didn't even know he was alive.'

'You believe his story?' asked Watson.

He glanced across at her. 'Didn't you?'

'I'm just trying to keep an open mind.'

'His story tallies with what the major told us.'

'They've had years to concoct a story,' Watson pointed out.

This time, Slater turned his head to study her face before he turned back to the road ahead. 'But you don't believe that any more than I do.'

'Good heavens, no,' she said. 'He convinced me, and I can't see the major being a party to anything like that. Anyway, it's like Hudson said, what other reason would he have had for coming to Trillington? If he just wanted to get arrested, for some bizarre reason, why not punch the first policeman he came across? Why create such an elaborate charade when you don't have to?'

Slater smiled to himself.

'And I'm no expert,' continued Watson, 'but he's not exactly classic murderer material, is he? He's far too gentle, even if he did get six months for assault.'

'He's certainly got more patience than me,' confessed Slater. 'I don't think I would have waited two weeks before I punched Norton, but I also think you're right about keeping an open mind. We can't rule anyone out just yet, but I think we can safely push David Hudson to the back of the queue.'

'Agreed,' said Watson.

'Of course we have two new suspects now,' said Slater.

'You mean Kylie's parents?' asked Watson. 'I don't know. Did they even know where Kylie was?'

'But she'd just had a baby. What if she wrote and told them they were grandparents?' asked Slater. 'That could have been a real red rag if they hated Hudson as much as he says. Or, even more provocative, what if she had turned up on their doorstep with a baby?'

Watson pulled a face.

'What's happened to keeping an open mind?' asked Slater. 'We can't ignore the possibility.'

'No, I suppose you're right about that, anything's possible.' She thought about this for a moment. 'What about this DS Norton? He doesn't sound like the most sympathetic officer you've ever met, does he? And it worries me that we know exactly when Hudson reported Kylie missing, yet we still couldn't find any report to back up his story.'

'Yeah, that's been nagging away at me, too,' admitted Slater. 'I think it's high time we had a little chat with Detective Sergeant Norton, his name seems to be cropping up all over the place.'

'There's another thing that concerns me,' said Watson. 'If Norton was right, and Kylie did run away with the baby, we have to assume she had somewhere to live, and that she went on to raise her son alone, or with someone else. If that's the case, and the body we found is the same child, why didn't Kylie report him missing? That doesn't sound like the caring mother that we've just been told about, does it?'

'I hate to say it, but people change,' said Slater. 'Who knows what might have happened in the intervening years. Maybe she died. Maybe she became some sort of smackhead and doesn't know what day it is.'

Watson gave him a look that could have been contempt, or perhaps pity.

'Yeah, I know,' he said, 'it's not a very nice thought, but it happens. You know it, we all know it.'

Watson picked up her mobile phone and thumbed through her contacts, lifting the phone to her ear once she had found the right one. 'We've got a name for the mother now,' she muttered as she waited for the call to connect. 'Let's see if the team can track her down.'

CHAPTER SIXTEEN

Because of Slater's pathological dislike of tunnels, Watson had been left with no choice but to book ferry tickets for their journey back across the channel too. It was as they neared the ferry terminal that Slater's mobile phone began to ring. It was Henry Cutter.

'Where are you?' Slater's phone was hands-free, and Henry's strident voice filled the car. 'I've been waiting all day to speak to you.'

'We're just queueing for the ferry back from France. We won't be home until the morning,' said Slater. 'What are you so excited about?'

'We thought it might be an idea to widen our search area around the initial burial site, just to see if we could find anything else to help you before we pack up and leave.'

'That means you did, right?'

'Yes, we did. It was such a tiny thing many of us might have missed the significance, but fortunately we have Nadira. She immediately recognised it as a distal phalange. That's your starter for ten.'

Slater looked at Watson, his face suitably ignorant.

'Isn't that a piece of finger?' asked Watson.

Cutter sounded impressed. 'Ten points to the young lady. It is indeed a piece of finger, the tip, to be precise.'

'Are you telling me you've found another body next to the first one?' asked a horrified Slater.

'It's another skeleton, and it wasn't quite that straightforward,' explained Cutter. 'It was actually about fifteen yards further along the ditch, but yes, we found another one.'

'Jesus, Henry,' said Slater. 'It's not another kid, is it? We're nowhere near finding out what happened to the first one yet!'

'We're not sure yet. It could be a child, or a small adult. Spoilt your day again, have I?' asked Cutter.

Slater sighed. 'I suppose that's your job, isn't it?' he said, with a rueful smile.

'Yes, I guess you could look at it like that.'

'So what can you tell us about this one?'

'We've only just got it out of the ground, so I can't tell you much except it's been down there for some years. We're going to work through, so we'll have something for you by the morning.'

'Don't overdo it,' said Slater. 'We won't be back until late morning. We've been driving all day, we're not driving through the night as well.'

'I've asked the lab to drop everything and rush the DNA sample.'

'You think the bodies could be related?' asked Slater.

'I have no idea,' said Cutter, noncommittally.

Slater sat up a bit straighter. 'But we could have a double murder on our hands.'

'I'm not saying anything of the sort, it's far too early to jump to that conclusion,' said Cutter, 'but it's always a possibility.'

'Right. We'll see you in the morning,' said Slater, ending the call. 'Bloody hell, Watson, what have we stumbled upon. A double murder?'

'Of course, it could just be two separate murders,' suggested Watson.

'Of course that's possible, too,' said Slater, thoughtfully, 'but I wonder what the chances are of two people dumping two bodies in exactly the same place.'

'Yes, when you put it like that it does seem a bit of a coincidence,' Watson conceded.

'We'll see,' said Slater, with a grim smile, 'but I'm not a great believer in coincidences.'

* * *

Slater had been calling Jenny every half hour for the last three hours, but it just kept going straight to voicemail. Either her phone was switched off, or she was somewhere where the signal was crap. He figured it was more likely to be the case that her phone was switched off. She could be very childish at times, and it would be typical of her to think frustrating him in this way would be a brilliant way of getting back at him. He left her one more message, this time suggesting that if she didn't call him back he wouldn't be calling her again, and then, feeling distinctly irritated he went to bed.

CHAPTER SEVENTEEN

'This new skeleton is that of a young woman,' announced Dr Henry Cutter next morning. 'We estimate she was around eighteen to twenty years old when she died.'

'So, are you saying these two were murdered together?' asked Slater.

'Well, I suppose it's quite logical to make that assumption,' said Cutter.

Slater looked suitably puzzled. 'But?'

'Well, I think we can rule out that particular possibility, because there is one peculiarity which calls that idea into question.' He nodded to Nadira.

'As you know, there's always a margin of error when it comes to estimating how long bodies have been in the ground,' she said, 'but even allowing for error, we're confident the bodies were buried at different times.'

'How different?' asked Slater.

'We estimate the young woman has been dead somewhere between fifteen and twenty years, and as you know, the child somewhere between six and ten years.'

'I'm not sure if that helps or simply complicates the issue,' said Slater, thoughtfully.

'There's more,' said Cutter, with a smile. 'Nadira thinks she may have a cause of death for the young woman, and this really should be a bit more helpful to you.'

'Really?' said Slater.

'Okay, so we know there may have been some damage from the JCB,' began Nadira. 'But actually there's not too much, and it's fairly easy to spot the recent damage. If you look here—' she pointed to the right leg where fractures were clearly visible both above and below the knee — 'you can see multiple fractures. These are old wounds that never got the chance to even start healing.'

'Which means they were caused at, or just before, the time of death,' Watson said.

'Exactly,' agreed Nadira. 'And the pelvis is fractured, and there are more here.' She pointed to further fractures to the ribs.

Slater had seen this sort of damage before. 'She was hit by a car,' he said.

Nadira nodded. 'I think so — and with extreme force. And if these injuries didn't kill her, this would have.' She finished by tilting the skull to reveal yet another fracture.

'Fractured skull where her head hit the bonnet?' suggested Watson.

'It could be that,' said Nadira, 'but she probably would have been thrown across the road, so it could have been impact with the road surface.'

'Do you think it happened on the road by the ditch?' asked Slater.

Nadira smiled. 'Now that's something I couldn't say. She could have been run down somewhere else and dumped here.'

There was a brief pause while they digested this latest bit of news.

'I'm sorry we can't tell you where she died, but we can tell you when,' said Cutter, brightly. 'We found her watch.'

He produced a clear plastic evidence bag with the watch inside, and passed it across to Slater, who studied the watch face and then passed it on to Watson.

'It says 22.45 on the night of 22 October,' announced Watson.

'I'm afraid we can't tell you the year,' said Cutter.

'Well, I'm disappointed,' said Slater, his tongue firmly in his cheek. 'I was rather hoping you were going to tell us the date and the make and model of the car.'

Cutter smiled back at him. 'Come now, we have to leave some work for the detectives!'

'So we have a young woman probably killed by a car, possibly a hit-and-run, and then a few years later a little boy may well have been strangled and dumped in the same ditch. If that's right, it's got to be the same killer, hasn't it?'

'I reckon that's your area of expertise, not ours,' said Cutter.

'So, if it was the same killer, they decided to bury the second body alongside the first,' mused Watson. 'But why would anyone do that?'

'Oh, that's easy,' said Slater. 'If you'd dumped a body ten years earlier and it was undiscovered, you'd be pretty sure you had a safe hiding place, wouldn't you?'

CHAPTER EIGHTEEN

'Is it me,' asked Watson when they were back in their own office, 'or is this case getting more and more confusing?'

'It's certainly getting more and more intriguing,' said Slater. 'I was the one who said if the first body had been undiscovered for ten years it would be a safe hiding place, but it wasn't, was it? Someone obviously knew that second body was there or there wouldn't have been a tip-off.'

'Someone must have seen the body being dumped,' Watson said, 'but why would you wait ten years before you reported it?'

'Blackmail?' said Slater. 'If you don't pay me every month I'm going to tell the police what you did?'

'But this was a child! Who would take cash to keep that quiet?'

'How long have you been a police officer?' asked Slater. 'That's a very naive attitude for someone with your experience. There are thousands of people who would put money before anything, and you should know it.'

Watson sighed. 'I suppose that's how I would like the world to be,' she admitted.

'It's how we'd all like it to be,' agreed Slater, 'but that would be more like an ideal world and, sadly, this is the real

74

world. Maybe someone defaulted on their payment and the tip-off was a warning. Maybe next time we'll get the name of the killer.'

Watson looked gloomy.

'Come on, Sam,' said Slater. 'We can't let our feelings get in the way or we won't be able to solve anything. Let's look at the timeline.'

'Right,' said Watson, determinedly. 'So we've got . . . Wait a minute! What if this young woman is Kylie Mason? What if David Hudson was right, and she didn't run away, but was hit by a car instead? He told us it was towards the end of October, in 2000, when she was supposed to have moved into the cottage. According to Dr Cutter her watch suggests she was killed at 22.45 on 22 October. If we assume she died where she was found, she could have been out walking the baby, trying to get him to sleep when someone ran her down.'

'Would you be out walking on these narrow country roads at night?' asked Slater, dubiously.

'Not normally, no,' agreed Watson, 'but don't forget she was only eighteen years old. She had just moved house, she was new to the area, she had a three-month-old baby, and Hudson said the baby didn't sleep well.'

Slater was trying to picture the scene. 'Go on,' he said, encouragingly.

'What if she had a baby who was screaming his head off, and she was at her wits' end and just desperate to get him off to sleep? She's got no one to turn to, but she knows walking seems to pacify the baby, so she puts on the sling, loads up the baby, and starts walking. She doesn't even think about where she's going, she just follows the footpath. She doesn't care about streetlights, she just wants to stop the baby crying. Don't forget, the footpath peters out just down the road. Perhaps she reached the end of the footpath and just kept walking on the road. Maybe she was so frazzled by the baby not sleeping, and by moving house, that she just didn't think.'

'Would she get that stressed?' asked Slater.

Watson gave him that look again, the one that could have been contempt or pity, he really couldn't tell. 'You don't know much about babies, do you, sir? I've known friends in their thirties with new babies, with a husband and grandparents on hand, and they still get so wound up they don't know what day of the week it is. We're talking about a girl of eighteen on her own with a new baby. She's still a kid herself, and she's just had to deal with moving house by herself. Of course she would have been stressed. I doubt the poor girl knew if she was coming or going!'

Slater figured the look must have been contempt after all but conceded the point. 'When you put it like that, it makes sense. So she walks along until she runs out of footpath, then has to walk in the road. So, why didn't she turn back?'

'She's desperate,' said Watson, 'and the baby's still crying. She daren't stop.'

'Okay, but it's dark and there are no streetlights. She could still turn around and go back to the village where there are lights.'

'But she's not thinking straight,' insisted Watson. 'Maybe she had a torch, or there was enough moonlight to see by.'

'Okay,' said Slater, thoughtfully, 'I'm with you so far. But if we assume the car coming towards her had headlights on, why didn't she see it coming and get out of the way?'

'That's a risky assumption,' argued Watson. 'What if the driver was drunk, he might not have had any lights on, or maybe they just weren't working for some reason. Besides, there's a bend at the top of that slope. Perhaps she didn't see it until it was too late.'

Slater thought for a minute. 'Or there was just nowhere for her to go to get out of the way,' he said. 'If she was going out of the village on the footpath, she would have been on the right side of the road, and there's no footpath on the other side to cross over to, so she probably would have stayed on that side. The thing is, that's where that bloody great ditch is. If it was dark, she couldn't risk stepping that way or she might have fallen in, and with the baby strapped to her she wouldn't risk that, would she?'

They both considered the scenario.

'And there's another possibility,' said Slater. 'I've been assuming the car was heading into the village. What if it was coming from the village?'

'It would have come up behind her,' said Watson.

'Exactly,' said Slater. 'And if she was on the right, there should have been plenty of room for it to have passed by on her left, but what if your theory is correct and the driver was drunk? Maybe he was going too fast, lost control, and didn't see Kylie until it was too late.'

'Nadira said she thought the car had hit her from the side, not the back,' Watson pointed out.

'Okay,' said Slater. 'So, Kylie's walking along, hears the car coming, but she thinks it's going to pass her by with plenty of room to spare. Then she hears something, maybe the car skids, or whatever, and she turns to see what's happening, and the car hits her as she's turning.'

'But what about the baby?' asked Watson.

'Maybe he's in that ditch and we just haven't found him yet,' Slater suggested. 'Or maybe Kylie is shielding the baby from a direct hit, and by some miracle he remains unhurt even when Kylie gets sent flying by the car.' He stared at Watson, who stared back but didn't speak. 'Well, what do you think?'

'I think, if it is Kylie Mason, it explains how she was killed, but what about the baby? Why haven't we found his body?'

'I dunno,' said Slater. 'Maybe we need to do another search of the ditch, but we don't even know for sure that this is Kylie Mason.'

'Could the driver have taken the baby?'

'If you're right, and this is Kylie, we have to consider that possibility,' he said. 'Unless, of course, there's still another tiny body to be found in that blessed ditch. We'll have to get Henry's team to check again.'

'If it is Kylie, we'll have to tell her parents,' said Watson.

'Hmm, yes, you're right. I wanted to speak to them anyway, but we'd best wait for the DNA results before we visit them. In the meantime, I want the team to continue searching for her, and I want her parents' address confirmed.'

'I'll chase them up,' said Watson.

'When you've done that, I think it's time we had a chat with DS Norton, don't you?'

'Oh yes, I'm going to enjoy that one,' said Watson, with a wicked grin.

'Good,' said Slater, 'because I want you to take the lead. Think you can handle it?'

'Yes, I think so.'

'Yes, so do I,' agreed Slater.

CHAPTER NINETEEN

'I'm DS Brearley, and this is DI Slater. We're from the Mobile Unsolved Case Unit.'

Norton sniffed his disgust. 'Never heard of it.'

'We're a new squad.'

'Oh! You mean you're one of these experimental Mickey Mouse units with nothing better to do than waste everybody else's time?'

'Actually,' said Watson, 'our main job is to try to solve old cases that went nowhere. You can call that a waste of time if you want to, but it's not how we see it.'

'You're all a waste of time,' said Norton. 'If it was down to me, we'd go back fifty years to the time when we could dish out a bit of justice for ourselves.'

Watson smiled sweetly at him. 'Maybe that's why you're still a DS,' she said. 'Dinosaurs never were the brightest species.'

Norton's face darkened. 'Who d'you think you're talking to?' he snapped.

'Oh, I know exactly who I'm talking to,' she said, stony-faced, 'but I'm not so sure you know who *you're* dealing with.'

Norton smiled at Slater. 'That's the trouble with these girls,' he said. 'They get ideas above their station—'

'Is that right?' said Slater, his voice icy. 'DS Brearley may be a woman, and she may be twenty years your junior, but she is your equal in rank. Ever think how something like that might have happened?' He gave Norton a split second to answer before continuing. 'No? Then let me tell you — it's because she is way ahead of you in brains, manners, professionalism, and just about anything else you care to mention. I can assure you I would rather have one of her working alongside me than ten of you. Now, you can give her the respect she deserves and we can keep this informal, or we can arrest you and make a big deal out of it. You choose.'

Norton licked his lips. Under the table, Slater noticed his right leg starting to twitch. 'What d'you mean arrest me? Arrest me for what? What's this about?'

'You look very nervous, Colin,' said Watson. 'Can I call you Colin? It's much friendlier, don't you think? What are you so nervous about?'

Norton swallowed hard. 'I'm not nervous, I'm fine. I've got nothing to worry about.'

'Oh right, that's good,' said Watson. 'Now, how good's your memory?'

'My memory's fine.'

'Wonderful,' said Watson. 'As I said before, part of our job is to look into old cases, and that's just what we're doing right now, just down the road, as it happens, in Trillington. You know Trillington? It's a nice little village a few miles outside town.'

'Of course I know it.'

Watson smiled at him. 'How about a man called David Hudson? Do you remember him?'

Norton adopted a look of puzzled innocence. 'No, can't say as I do. The name's not ringing any bells.'

'I wouldn't be surprised if the bells have rusted solid,' said Watson, quietly.

'What's that?'

'I said I'm surprised,' said Watson. 'There can't be that many men who've laid you out over the years, although I bet there have been plenty who wanted to.' She picked a sheet of paper out from the file in front of her. 'David Hudson,' she read, 'was convicted of assaulting a police officer in March 2001. He got six months. You were the officer he assaulted.'

'Oh, *him*,' said Norton. 'Yeah, now you come to mention it, I do remember him. He was a nutter, punched me for no reason.'

'Is that right?' asked Watson. 'It says here the magistrate thought he had good reason for thumping you. He only sentenced him because he had no choice. What do you say to that?'

'What does a magistrate know? Sitting there like God, telling us how to do our jobs. I mean, what does he know? When did he ever have to deal with a nutcase like Hudson?'

'You keep saying he's a nutcase,' said Watson, 'but he seemed sane enough when we spoke to him the other day. Did you ever check his story out?'

'Of course I did.'

'Are you sure?' asked Watson. 'Tell me about it.'

'Gawd, I can't remember. That was years and years ago.'

'He came in to report his girlfriend and their baby were missing, does that help?'

'Why are you asking me? If they were missing, there would be a report. Why don't you look at that? It'll all be in there.'

'You mean the missing person report?' asked Watson, who was really warming to her job now. 'Well, I'd love to, but you see, that's the thing that makes me think you didn't do your job. There is no report.'

'But there was no missing person!' snapped Norton. 'When I went to the cottage where he claimed she was living, the people there had never heard of her.'

'That's funny,' said Watson. 'First you couldn't remember Hudson, and then you did. Then you didn't remember anything about the case, and now you do. What's going on here, Colin?'

'What does it matter? It was years ago.'

'It matters because we're the team investigating the child's body that was found in a ditch just outside Trillington,' said Watson. 'Well, it wasn't really a body, he'd been there so long there were only his bones left. DNA testing proves David Hudson was the father. It's actually quite lucky he punched you in the face, or we wouldn't have had his DNA on file and we probably never would have known who the father was.'

Norton's face was ashen, a picture of confusion. His eyes seemed to dart everywhere, but he couldn't look either of them in the face.

'So you see where we're going with this, don't you, Colin?' asked Watson. 'If you had done your job back then, and taken David Hudson seriously, maybe you would have found his girlfriend and her baby. Perhaps they might even have still been alive. Perhaps they might still be alive today!'

Watching Norton from alongside Watson, Slater got the impression Norton's mind was on something else, although he couldn't quite put his finger on why he thought that.

'I've already told you, I went to the cottage and there was no sign of her,' pleaded Norton.

'Did you check with the landlord?' asked Watson.

'Eh?'

'The landlord,' asked Watson. 'You know, the person who owns the cottage and rents it out.'

'I dunno. I'm sure I would have, but I told you, I can't remember.'

'I think you *can* remember,' said Watson, 'but you're choosing not to tell us the whole story.'

'Look,' he said, finally beginning to get a grip on his composure. 'I thought the bloke was a time-waster, right? I mean he comes to us in December saying she disappeared in October. Why did he wait two months to tell us?'

'Don't you know?' asked Watson. 'If you had done your job properly, you would have known he was in the army. He had just come back from a six-month posting! Surely you asked him?'

'I can't remember everything.'

'Well, I think you'd better start remembering something, Colin, because right now your selective memory is beginning to get on my nerves. I don't know why you decided to treat David Hudson the way you did, but there's no doubt you didn't do your job. We're supposed to be here to help people, but you didn't help him, did you?'

'Look, I thought he was a chancer. If this girlfriend *did* exist, it seemed pretty obvious to me that she had taken the guy for a ride and cleared off with someone else. I even told him so.'

Watson aimed a mirthless smile in his direction. 'Yes, I know. And you told him you thought her baby wasn't his, didn't you? That's why he punched your lights out.'

Norton was licking his lips again, and the leg twitch tempo had increased to twice the original pace. 'Have we finished?' he asked, almost defiantly.

'I have,' said Watson. She looked at Slater. 'Have you anything to add, sir?'

Slater smiled his best crocodile smile. 'Of course, you would have recorded your encounters with Hudson in your notebook, wouldn't you, DS Norton?'

'I can't recall,' he said, sullenly, 'but I think I would have, yes.'

'Even though you didn't write a full report?'

Norton looked uncertain, thought about it for a moment, and then gave Slater a sly smile. 'I'm sure I would have recorded it in my notebook, sir.'

'Oh, good. In that case I'd like to see that notebook.'

Norton's smile widened to a grin. 'That must have been nearly twenty years ago. I'm sure it would have been destroyed by now.'

Slater grinned back at him. 'You would have thought so, wouldn't you,' he said, 'and in a lot of forces it would have been, but we checked with your records office. Luckily for us, your force is one of those that keeps everything for twenty-five years.'

The smile faded rapidly from Norton's face. Suddenly he didn't look quite so clever.

'I'd like to see that notebook,' said Slater.

'But—'

'Don't argue with me, DS Norton. That's not a request, it's an order, understand?'

'Yes. Sir. Can I go now?'

'Yes, but you should be aware we know you're hiding something,' said Slater. 'We don't know what it is yet, but I promise you we're going to find out, and when we do I'm going to come down on you like a ton of bricks. Now, get out of my sight, and don't forget I want to see that notebook.'

Slater watched in disgust as Norton scuttled from the room. 'How do you feel?' he asked Watson.

'Sordid,' she said. 'I think I need a shower.'

'Yes, he's not the most pleasant, is he?'

'How can he live with himself?'

'No conscience,' said Slater. 'You can understand why Hudson lumped him one, can't you? I wanted to.'

'There's a queue,' said Watson. 'And I claim the first punch.'

Slater laughed and gave her a ready smile. 'Only if I can watch,' he said.

CHAPTER TWENTY

Watson clicked 'print' and swung her chair round. She stopped halfway round to grab the two sheets of paper spewing from the printer, then continued swinging round until she was facing Slater. 'I've got some updates,' she said.

He swung his own chair round to face her. 'Fire away.'

'First, the St Christopher pendant: they've confirmed the hallmark belongs to Edmond Moynihan, a Dublin silversmith who started producing silver artefacts towards the end of the nineteenth century and on into the twentieth century through his son. Apparently there is still a jewellers bearing the Moynihan name, and the good news is, they have records going back donkey's years. They say the pendant was their own design and was produced during a period either side of the turn of the century.'

'I don't suppose they have a list of buyers?' asked Slater.

'I'm afraid the records aren't that good, but they did say they thought there were unlikely to have been more than a few hundred made.'

Slater sighed. 'Well, it's not proof, but it's a start,' he said. 'I mean, what are the chances two little boys of similar age would be wearing the same pendant, when less than a thousand were ever made? If only we could find a way of linking Diana Randall to Dublin.'

'I could ask them to check further into her family background,' suggested Watson.

'I suppose it wouldn't hurt,' agreed Slater, trying to sound a bit more optimistic than he felt.

Watson had her notebook balanced on her knee. She made a quick note before continuing with her updates. 'They can't find any trace of Kylie Mason after October 2000. Up until then she was living in a flat in Winchester, but after that she just disappears without trace.'

'That would tie in with what David Hudson told us,' said Slater. 'He said she was in a flat before they got the cottage, but where the hell did she go after that?'

He thought for a moment, mulling everything over. Watson stayed silent, as if she could see the cogs turning in his head.

'Can you ask them to see if they can find her medical records, Sam? I think it's probably safe to assume she didn't have her baby at home on her own, so there must be a record of that little boy's birth somewhere in the Winchester area. And ask them to check with the local registry office to see if they can find a birth certificate.'

'That shouldn't be a problem,' she said, adding another note to her list. 'Next on the list are Kylie's parents. The team has confirmed they are still living at the same address.'

'Let's wait until we have the DNA results before we go and see them,' said Slater. 'We'll look like a pair of idiots if we have to go twice.'

'I've also had the guys looking for any road traffic accidents, or hit-and-run reports, involving a young woman, or a young woman and baby, on or around the latter part of October, but so far they've found nothing that looks likely.'

'How wide's the search?'

'I told them fifty miles.'

'I would have thought that would be wide enough,' agreed Slater. He gave her an encouraging smile. 'That's good work. It sounds like you've covered just about everything.'

'There is one other thing,' she said, a little apprehensively. 'You didn't ask me, but I thought it might be an idea to see if we can find the landlord for the cottage in Trillington, the one that Kylie was supposed to have been living in.'

'One step ahead,' said Slater, appreciatively. 'I like that.' He was genuinely impressed with Watson's initiative. He had known from the brief period he'd worked with her before that she was competent, but he was now beginning to realise just how efficient she really was, and how much harder his life would be without her here. He was lucky to have her alongside him, and he knew it. 'And what did you find?'

Looking immensely pleased with herself, she held the third sheet of paper up for him to see, a big smile on her face. 'You name it, we've got it. Name, address, DoB, I can even tell you his business is called Country Cottage Holdings, and his offices are no more than ten minutes from here, at the other end of Trillington.'

Slater smiled at her pleasure. He'd briefly forgotten they were in a small mobile office under a barn on a farm just outside the tiny village of Trillington so, of course, she was right; it would only take a few minutes to get there.

'In that case,' he said, 'we'd better go and see him.'

CHAPTER TWENTY-ONE

As Watson had said, Country Cottage Holdings was situated at the far end of the village, housed in a converted barn in the grounds of an expensive-looking house. Slater didn't know much about buildings or architecture, but the house didn't look very old and he guessed it had probably been built in the nineties.

The staff of Country Cottage Holdings consisted of the owner, Howard Glossop, and his secretary, Rosemary, who also happened to be his wife. Over the years they had managed to take ownership of some twenty rental properties, from which they made a very healthy monthly income. They were both in their sixties and appeared to be enjoying a comfortable existence without a care in the world. They had raised a son and daughter who had now moved on to live their own lives, and it seemed the Glossops were coasting towards a happy retirement.

'Good afternoon,' said Slater as he walked into the comfortable reception area. A small, slender, silver-haired lady sitting at the only desk in the room gave him a welcoming smile. Slater thought it rather strange he was immediately reminded of his mother, whom he hadn't seen, or spoken to, in months.

Her welcoming smile quickly evaporated, however, when he showed her his warrant card. 'I'm Detective Inspector Slater, and this is Detective Sergeant Brearley. We'd like to speak to Howard Glossop.'

'I'm Rosemary Glossop. My husband's on a telephone call at the moment. I'm sure he won't be long. Maybe I can help in the meantime?'

Slater gave her a reassuring smile. 'We're looking into the disappearance of a young woman back in 2000. We understand she, and her future husband, had leased a cottage from Country Cottage Holdings in October that year. We're trying to ascertain if this is correct, and if she ever actually moved in.'

'I'm sorry, I'm not going to be much help,' she said, with an embarrassed smile. 'I wasn't working here in 2000. The business was much smaller then, and I was at home raising the children.' Just as she finished speaking, a door opened off to one side, and a man's voice could be heard before he poked his head around it.

'Could you make me a cup of tea, Rosie?' Then he noticed Slater and Watson. 'Oh, sorry, I didn't know you had company.'

'I don't have company,' she said. 'You're the one with company, Howard It's the police, they've come to see you.'

'Me? Why would they want to see me?'

'How would I know? I expect one of your dodgy deals has backfired or something. Why don't you invite them into your office, and ask them?' she snapped.

The man had manoeuvred halfway through the open door now. He was red-faced and sweating profusely. Large enough to make Slater's former partner, Norman Norman, look relatively slim, he was in shirtsleeves, the top button of his trousers undone, and with the zip fly looking in imminent danger of giving up the struggle. Slater didn't think braces ever looked good on anyone, but at least in this case he could see they served a purpose. He looked at Rosemary Glossop again, and then back at her husband, and wondered about their relationship. She had looked quite happy and serene until he had appeared, but now she looked anything but.

'You'd better come through,' said Howard. He turned sideways on so Watson would have to squeeze past, but she was wise to the ways of dirty old men who wanted to rub up against her, and after shaping to pass him, she settled for stepping on his toes as heavily as she could, then stepped back and glared at him. He looked guiltily at Slater, who pursed his lips and inclined his head. 'Really? In front of your wife?'

Rosemary sat at her desk, colour rising rapidly to her cheeks. From the look on her face, Slater wondered if she hoped they would arrest him and take him away to teach him a lesson.

'Pull up a chair,' offered the even more red-faced Howard Glossop as he closed the door behind them. He shuffled across to his desk as quickly as his bulk would allow and tried to ease himself into the leather chair behind his huge desk but failed miserable and dropped into it instead. The chair made a couple of sweaty, squeaky, fart-like noises as he slumped into it. Slater caught Watson's eye as they each dragged a chair across to the desk. She looked horrified and obviously wasn't convinced it was Glossop's chair the noises had come from.

'Now then, what can I do for you?' Glossop asked.

'As I told your wife, we're investigating the disappearance of a young woman in 2000.'

'In 2000? Are you serious? It's a bit bloody late now, isn't it?' asked Howard, sarcastically. 'Have you got nothing better to do?'

'To be honest I'd quite like to be arresting disgusting, dirty old men using any opportunity to rub themselves up against the nearest woman,' snapped Watson, 'but unfortunately we have to prioritise what we do.'

Glossop looked like he had an angry response on the tip of his tongue, but he caught Slater's expression and clearly thought better of it.

'As DS Brearley says, we have to prioritise,' said Slater, pointedly. 'And since you mentioned the word serious, I should point out nothing is more serious to us than murder.'

'Murder?' asked Howard, not sounding quite so full of himself now. 'So what are you doing here? I've not murdered anyone.'

'I should hope not.' said Slater.

'Anyway, I don't see how I can help,' said Glossop. 'I was far too busy building this business in 2000 to be worrying about missing women, and like I said, I've never murdered anyone. I think I'd remember, don't you?' He smiled at his own little joke, but neither of the two detectives smiled back.

'Perhaps your wife will remember?'

'No chance,' said Glossop. 'She has no idea about the business, and anyway she wasn't working here back then, she was at home looking after the kids.' It appeared he fully expected Slater and Watson to leave at this point, but when it became obvious they weren't going to, he added, 'Anyway, if that's all, I'm a busy man, and I'm sure you've got better things to do than waste my time.'

He gave Slater a thin smile, but all he got in return was a fixed, icy smile that gave off no warmth whatsoever.

'Have you got a glass of water?' asked Watson. 'I've got a very dry throat.'

'Not in here, you'll have to ask Rosemary,' said Glossop, grudgingly.

'Thank you,' said Watson with a sweet smile. 'I'll go and ask her.'

Slater waited until she had left the room before he spoke. 'How much pornography would we find on that computer of yours, Mr Glossop?' he asked.

'What?' Glossop's body gave a sudden jerk and the colour slowly drained from his face. 'I don't know what you're talking about.'

'No, of course you don't,' said Slater, wearily. 'So you'd be happy for DS Brearley to take a look, would you?'

'You can't do that. Anyway, there's a password.'

'That won't stop us,' said Slater. 'We'll just take it away and hand it to our technical nerd unit. They'll crack it in five minutes.'

Glossop stared at Slater, a sheen of sweat on his brow.

'Now listen to me, Mr Glossop,' said Slater. 'You seem to think this young woman's death should be of no interest to anyone, that it's some sort of joke. I bet you'd be interested in her if she was in this room and you thought you could get your dirty hands on her, wouldn't you?'

'Now, listen here,' said Glossop, indignantly. 'You can't talk to me like this.'

'You think I'm wasting your time now,' hissed Slater. 'Well, let me tell you, I haven't even started yet. I bet if we went through your business we would find all sorts of fiddles going on, and as for that computer, well, I would be willing to bet there's enough porn on there to keep all your mates in prison happy for a long, long time.'

'What? What mates in prison? I don't know anyone in prison.'

'Not yet,' said Slater, 'but by the time we've finished you'll have the opportunity to make friends with a whole prison-full.'

'You can't. You've got no grounds to do any of that.'

'D'you want to try me?'

Slater stared hard at Glossop who swallowed hard and looked away. 'But why do you think I can help?' he whined.

'Because she was supposed to be coming to live in Trillington around the time she went missing,' said Slater. 'She and her husband-to-be had leased one of your cottages.'

'Can I just stop you there,' said Glossop. 'I think I would remember if one of my tenants had gone missing. This is a reputable business, you know. We look after our tenants.'

'I take it you keep records?' asked Slater.

'What, back to 2000? I don't think we've still got that stuff,' said Glossop confidently. 'It would have been destroyed years ago. I'm sorry, but I can't help you. It's not that I don't want to.'

Slater knew Glossop was trying to rush him out through the door, so he obviously had something to hide, and it wasn't just the porn on his computer. He hoped Watson was doing what he thought she was doing. Slowly and reluctantly, he allowed Glossop to talk down to him and usher him to the door. As Glossop followed Slater through the door into reception, Watson and Rosemary Glossop looked up. They were both behind Rosemary's desk, studying her computer screen.

'It looks like Mrs Glossop knows a bit more about the business than Mr Glossop realises,' said Watson. 'And she thought it might be prudent to computerise all their old records before they were destroyed.'

Slater turned an icy smile towards Glossop, who had stopped dead in his tracks, mouth gaping in shock. 'Perhaps you'd better sit down before you fall down, Mr Glossop,' he said, pointing to a couple of chairs off to one side. 'So, what have you found?' asked Slater as he walked across to the desk.

'According to this, a Mr and Mrs Hudson paid a month's rent in advance as a deposit and took a lease on a cottage in Trillington. The lease started from 20 October 2000, but then on 20 November 2000, a Mr Higgs took over the lease.'

Slater turned to Glossop. 'Does that ring any bells? If she was there, what happened to her stuff?'

Glossop pointed a finger at Rosemary. 'She's made a mistake,' he said. 'She made a good little wife, but she's as good as useless with paperwork.'

'It all looks pretty good to me,' said Watson. 'I think the problem's more likely to be your attitude, not your wife's abilities.'

'Mr Glossop?' asked Slater.

'I told you, I don't remember.'

'Well, I suggest you start remembering,' said Slater.

'Now, wait a minute—'

'No, *you* wait a minute,' said Slater. 'You've been treating this like a joke up until now, but I don't think you understand the situation you're in. We have a murder victim who disappeared within two days of taking out a lease with you. In our book, that makes you a murder suspect.'

'This can't be happening,' said Glossop, in disbelief. 'You can't do this.'

'It looks like we *are* doing it,' said Slater. 'It's just a question of where. You can either start remembering here and now, or we can call the local nick and have you dragged off to a cell until we find time to question you.'

'Yes, please,' muttered Rosemary Glossop, loud enough for everyone to hear.

'You're supposed to be my wife,' Glossop said angrily. 'What happened to family loyalty? You'd be lost without me!'

'Oh, please,' she said, scornfully. 'I've been running this business for the past five years. How do you think everything gets done when all you do is drool over that damned computer all day long?'

'I do nothing of the sort!'

'Yes, you do,' she said. 'I've seen the websites you're logged onto. I'm not the idiot you think I am.'

'But I've got a password—'

'Yes, but you haven't got the wit to use anything worthwhile. How long do you think it took me to work out it was my name and your birthday? I know why you won't tell the inspector what happened to the girl's belongings. It's got something to do with that Jacko, hasn't it?'

'Shut up, you stupid bitch!' Glossop shouted.

Slater fished his mobile phone from his pocket and turned to him. 'Who's Jacko, Mr Glossop? Or, would you prefer it if I make the phone call?'

'It's not what you think.'

'So, tell me what it is,' said Slater. He waited a few seconds as he searched his contacts and then pressed the dial key and raised the phone to his ear.

Glossop stared at Slater, his mouth hanging open.

Slater heard the call connect in his ear, and the familiar voice began to speak. 'At the third stroke . . .'

'Hello,' he said into the phone, 'this is DI Slater.'

Glossop held up his hands. 'All right, I'll talk,' he gasped. 'Just, please, don't make me spend a night in a cell.'

Slater gave him that icy smile again and ended his call. 'There, that wasn't such a hard decision to make was it? Now, why don't we all sit down and then you can tell us all about it.'

'Good idea,' said Rosemary. 'I can't wait!'

Watson took a seat at Rosemary's desk so she could take notes, and Slater pulled three more chairs over. 'There,' he said with an evil grin once he was happy with the set-up. 'Isn't this cosy?'

Glossop slumped miserably into one of the chairs. 'It was a long time ago,' he said. 'I can't promise I can recall all the details.'

'Don't start making excuses before you've even started,' said Slater, 'because if I think you're giving us a load of crap, I'll make that call again, but this time I'll finish it.'

'No, no,' pleaded Glossop, his face a picture of misery. 'I promise I'll tell you everything I can remember.'

'Right then,' said Slater, 'let's start with the lease.' He nodded to Watson, who read from the computer screen.

'It says here the Hudsons were due to move in on 20 October, and the lease was for a minimum term of six months.'

'That would be correct,' said Glossop. 'That's how we've always worked. The first six months is like a trial period, but as long as a tenant pays up on time and takes reasonable care of the property, they can stay for as long as they want.'

'So what happened with the Hudsons?' asked Slater. 'If you re-let the cottage on 20 November that means they weren't even in there for one month.'

'They paid a month up front as a deposit, and then they were supposed to pay monthly starting on 30 October.'

'And?'

'And nothing. They never paid.'

'So you kicked them out?'

'No, I went round to find out why they hadn't paid.'

'Did you know Mr Hudson was in the army?'

'Yes.'

'So you could have gone to his CO and complained he wasn't paying. You know what happens then, don't you? The

CO would kick Hudson's arse all over camp and then arrange for you to be paid before he even got his wages. The army don't approve of that sort of thing, it gets them a bad name.'

'I had heard something like that, but it never got that far.'

'Did you know the young woman, Kylie, had just had a baby and was going to be moving in and living on her own for the first couple of months?'

'Like I said, I knew he was in the army, but they didn't tell me she was moving in on her own.'

'Did they tell you they weren't actually married yet?'

'No, they didn't, nor that she was pregnant.' He managed to sound indignant.

'Would that have been a problem if you had known?'

'No, it wouldn't,' said Rosemary before he could answer. 'He's a hypocrite if he says otherwise. I only married him because I was foolish enough to get pregnant.'

Slater looked at Glossop. 'Well?'

He shrugged unhappily. 'No, I don't think it would have been a problem.'

'Right,' said Slater, 'so did they, or at least did Kylie, move in on 20 October?'

'I suppose she must have.'

'What do you mean "I suppose she must have"?'

'Well, I left the place unlocked and keys inside, so I didn't actually see her move in, but I know she must have.'

'You're sure about this?' asked Slater, patiently. 'Only this is very important. Up until now, we only have Mr Hudson's word that she had moved in, and of course, he couldn't know for sure because he was in Kosovo.'

'I know she did because when I went round there to get my money, there was no sign of her, but her stuff was there.'

'You're sure about that?'

'Yes.'

'So what happened to her stuff? Only the people who moved in after her said the place was empty.'

'Of course it was empty,' said Glossop, testily. 'I couldn't let a property with the previous tenant's belongings still there, could I?'

Slater studied Glossop for a few seconds. 'I don't think you're in a position to start getting stroppy with me, Howard. You should be aware you've just told us you had a motive for murdering Kylie, so if I were you, instead of trying to piss me off, I'd start thinking about how you could make me happy.'

Glossop looked stunned at the idea that he could possibly have a motive for murder.

'She owed you money,' explained Watson. 'You went round there, got angry, and killed her.'

'You can't think I would do that!' said Glossop.

'Of course we can,' said Slater.

'It's one possible scenario,' added Watson. 'Why don't you give us another one? Tell us your version of what happened.'

'But she wasn't there,' he pleaded. 'I thought she must be out so I went back the next day, and the next, but she was never there. This went on for about a week, but it was obvious she wasn't using the place. I looked in the fridge and there was nothing to eat. I looked around, but most of her stuff was still in boxes. I couldn't find anything that told me what was going on. I asked the neighbours, but no one had seen her. They didn't even know she had moved in.'

'So what did you do, go to the police?'

'Well, no,' he said, sheepishly. 'I just assumed she'd changed her mind and run off. You know how flighty these young people are.'

'Did you ever meet her?' asked Slater.

'Well, no.'

'Yet you're able to judge her character?'

'Err, well, I just thought—'

'Yeah, right, you "just thought". Didn't you tell us earlier you looked out for your tenants? You don't seem to have looked out for young Kylie, do you?'

Glossop bowed his head but said nothing.

'So what *did* happen to her stuff? And who's this Jacko? What does he have to do with it?'

'Jacko buys and sells stuff,' said Rosemary, glaring at her husband's bowed head. 'I bet you sold her stuff to him, didn't you?'

He looked up at her and nodded his head slowly.

'Oh, wonderful,' said Slater.

'There were clothes and shoes and things. And lots of baby stuff. It was worth a few quid, you know. I was just trying to get back what I was owed.'

'You had a deposit!' shrieked Rosemary, angrily. 'I can't believe you. You've gone too far this time!'

'So, you sold all her stuff without ever wondering what might have happened to her,' said Slater, shaking his head in disgust. 'Oh, Howard, what a caring person you are. Well, here's something for you to think about. While you were busying scraping a few quid together from her belongings, which is theft by the way, the poor girl hadn't had second thoughts and run off. She was lying at the bottom of that bloody great deep ditch just outside the village. She'd been hit by a car. It's possible she might even have still been alive at that point.'

'Oh, God help us, Howard, what have you done?' whispered Rosemary.

Slater got to his feet. 'Come on, Sam, I think I've heard enough, let's get out of here.' He turned to Rosemary Glossop, 'I'm sorry, Mrs Glossop.'

'No, Inspector, I'm the one who's sorry.' She glared at Howard. 'And him,' she spat. 'I'm so very, very ashamed of him.'

Watson got to her feet and followed after Slater, but before she got to the door she turned back. 'One more thing, Mr Glossop, did the local police ever speak to you about this matter. If not at the time, then maybe a couple of months later?'

Glossop slowly raised his tear-streaked face to her and shook his head. 'No, never,' he said.

'Right, thank you,' she said and then followed after Slater.

* * *

'I'm sorry about that,' said Slater, as he started the car.

Watson turned towards him. 'About what? D'you mean the dirty old man? Don't worry, I've had to deal with a lot worse than pathetic specimens like him. I was tempted to make use of the bionic knee and whack him in the balls, but he wouldn't have been much use to us if I had. Besides, that would have meant touching him.' She wrinkled her nose in distaste. 'I'm afraid it goes with the territory, ask any woman. I suppose I'm even more of a grope magnet being a police officer. I suppose it must be double the thrill.'

Slater thought he would have quite liked to see how the bionic knee stood up to the test, but he didn't tell her that. 'Yeah, but it's not right. You shouldn't have to put up with that sort of thing.'

'Don't worry, boss, I can deal with it,' she said, with a grim smile. 'Besides, I think he's just crossed a line where his wife's concerned. I suspect she's turned a blind eye for years, but he's just humiliated her in front of us, and that was probably a step too far. She's going to make his life hell for that.'

'Let's hope so,' said Slater, as he pulled away. 'Anyway, do we believe anything he told us?'

'I think he was probably telling the truth because he was terrified we were going to take his computer and find all his porn.'

'Yeah, that's what I thought,' agreed Slater. 'And I think he's too much of a coward to tell any lies we can easily check out, in case we come back and carry out the threat.'

'Should we have found out who this Jacko is?' she asked.

'Maybe,' he admitted, 'but I think we've probably found out all we needed to know, and if we do feel the need to speak to that guy, we now know a man who can put us in touch.'

Watson pulled a face. 'I suppose so,' she said, 'if we really have to. But if he tries that creepy stuff again—'

'Then you have my permission to test the knee to the maximum,' said Slater.

Watson looked at Slater in surprise.

'Don't look so surprised,' he said. 'If the guy took a swing at you, I wouldn't expect you to just stand there and be assaulted. In my view this is the same thing. It might be a different type of assault in the eyes of the law, but it's still an assault, and in that case you're entitled to act in self-defence.'

'That's a refreshing point of view,' said Watson, turning back to face the front.

'I like to be different.'

'I think we've definitely established that, sir,' she agreed.

Slater smiled. 'Good, I'm pleased to hear it.'

* * *

It was eight o'clock by the time Slater checked his phone, but there was nothing from Jenny. No missed call, no message, nothing. He thought about calling her, but then remembered what he had said in the last message he had left her. He decided there was no point in making the threat and then not carrying it out, so he put his phone down and turned on the TV.

CHAPTER TWENTY-TWO

Slater dropped Watson off at the office next morning and drove off to attend to some personal things promising he would be back a little later. To his surprise, when he did get back, there was no sign of Watson, and there was no note to tell him where she was. He tried the MAFU lab, but she wasn't there either, so he resorted to calling her mobile phone.

'Where are you? I was beginning to wonder if I'd driven you away.'

'If that's what you're trying to do, you'll have to try harder,' she said. 'You said last night you were still waiting for Norton to produce his notebook, so I thought I'd try and speed things up.'

'I bet he was pleased to see you.'

'I didn't waste my breath on *him*,' she said. 'I thought he'd probably just make another excuse to keep us waiting, so I went straight to the records office and asked them myself.'

'Ha! I've been in one of those county headquarters vaults. I know what they're like. I bet they told you it's in there somewhere, but they have no idea where.'

'Actually, Ramlinstoke keep their own records, and they do quite a good job of keeping everything in order. It's taken me a couple of hours, and I'm covered in dust and grime, but I found what I was looking for in the end. I'm just going to the hotel for a shower and to get some clean clothes, and then I'll be back.'

Once again, Slater found himself admiring Watson's attitude. A lot of DSs would have accepted Norton's excuses and kept on waiting, but she obviously wasn't one for messing around, and she didn't mind getting her hands dirty. There was no doubt she was going to keep him on his toes, and he actually liked that idea.

He turned his attention to his email inbox. It hadn't taken him long to discover that now he was a DI, the majority of his messages were basically circulars sent to all officers of his rank and above. These he now forwarded to 'DI Garbage', which wasn't a person but a folder he had created specially for the purpose, where they remained, unloved, unopened and unwanted. But among all this dross, he was pleased to see that at least there was one message that might be worth opening. It was from his boss, Detective Superintendent Bradshaw, and it concerned former DI Diana Randall.

As he quickly read through the message, his mouth dropped open in surprise, then he smiled to himself and read it again. He got up from his desk, made a cup of tea in the tiny kitchen, returned to his desk, and read the message again. The message confirmed Diana Randall had been working as a DS at Ramlinstoke before she was promoted to DI and moved up to Flipton. So Diana had a connection to Ramlinstoke, where both bodies had been found, and she had chosen not to tell them. Slater figured this was definitely food for thought.

According to Bradshaw, and this was the reason Slater had been surprised, the official reason for Diana Randall's resignation from the force had been depression. Slater smiled to himself again. The way Bradshaw had worded the message told him there was more to this than met the eye, and the additional information that there had been 'unconfirmed rumours about an affair with another officer' suggested what he might look for.

A small 'ping' from his laptop announced the arrival of another email. To his surprise, it was another from his boss. He clicked on the message and read it through. This new message suggested he should seek out a retired desk sergeant called Ted Rivers for further information.

As he sipped his tea, he allowed himself a few moments of idle speculation, but his thoughts soon turned to feelings of guilt. He wondered if there was any way a possible affair could be relevant to their inquiry, or was it more the case that he wanted to find some dirt on Diana Randall simply because he didn't much like her? And anyway, who was he to adopt this 'holier than thou' attitude, and judge her? Hadn't he done the very same thing himself and had a brief, unwise fling with his previous boss?

He tried to justify his position by telling himself that it was different because in his case they had both been single, and no one else had been hurt, but it didn't really make him feel any less of a hypocrite. He was still struggling with his guilty conscience when Watson returned, carrying a dusty old archive box which she dumped unceremoniously in the middle of the floor, creating a small cloud of dust in the process. Her white latex gloves were a grubby grey colour.

'Good grief,' said Slater, looking down at the box. 'No wonder you needed to go and get changed!' A hand-shaped smudge through the dust on the lid showed where Watson had checked the index when she had found the box.

'I had to sign for the whole box but, according to the index, Norton's notebooks for December 2000 are in here.'

Slater made to ask the next question, but she beat him to it. 'And, before you ask, yes, I did look inside to make sure. I also checked the log to see if anyone else had been down in the archive looking for this box recently, but you can see from the state of it that no one's been near it in years.'

'So, if Norton's made no attempt to find the notebook, what does that tell us?' asked Slater, thinking out loud. 'Does it suggest he's just a lazy arse and hasn't bothered, or does it suggest he thought I was bluffing?'

'I would imagine he's the sort who wouldn't want to go down in that archive, especially if it meant getting filthy. I bet he was hoping we were going to go away before it came to that. Of course, it could be he's got nothing to hide and he resents having to prove it.'

Slater studied Watson's face. 'Yeah, right, but you don't believe that any more than I do. Anyway, resent it or not, we all have to prove our intentions now and then. No one likes it, but it goes with the job.'

'I'm not defending him,' said Watson, 'I'm just saying how he might be thinking. Don't forget, if the chip on your shoulder's big enough, it affects your view.'

Slater smiled at that comment. 'It did seem pretty big, didn't it? More like a boulder than a chip.'

'Maybe it's a bluff on his part,' Watson suggested. 'Perhaps he thinks if he doesn't go near it, we'll think there's nothing to find and we won't bother looking.'

Slater laughed as he snapped on a pair of latex gloves. 'In that case, let's call his bluff and see what we've got.' He flexed his fingers theatrically as he stepped towards the box, then he lifted the lid and looked inside. To his surprise, everything inside was bundled and labelled, and it took just a few seconds to find Norton's notebooks.

'Right then, let's see what we've got,' he said, as he carefully lifted the bundle of notebooks from the box and placed them on his desk. There were just two notebooks that covered December, so they took one each and settled at their desks. It soon became apparent Norton used his own version of shorthand, which Slater thought wasn't going to make things easy for them, but then he realised names and addresses were written in longhand. As he was basically looking for names, maybe it wouldn't be so hard after all. In fact, it might even make things a little easier.

Fittingly, as she was the one who had used her initiative to get hold of the notebooks, it was Watson who found the first entry relating to David Hudson. 'Here we are,' she said. 'David Hudson, 15 December 2000.'

Slater left his own desk and crossed to Watson's desk, where he peered over her shoulder. 'Can you read his shorthand?' asked Slater. 'I can barely make head nor tail of it.'

'It's not easy,' she agreed, 'and the scrawled handwriting definitely doesn't help!' She studied the page for a minute. 'I think it says at 22.00 David Hudson reported his girlfriend and their baby missing. The address of the cottage is there too.' She flipped a page and studied it for another minute or so. 'Right, now it's the next morning. He's been out to the cottage, but the people there are called Higgs, and they've never heard of anyone called Hudson. There's a date here, 20 November.'

'That was the date the Higgs family moved in,' said Slater. 'But why does he say they've never heard of anyone called Hudson? Why isn't he asking about Kylie Mason? That was her name.'

Watson scanned the page again, flipped back to the previous page, and scanned again. 'He hasn't taken her name,' she said in surprise. 'There's no mention of Kylie anywhere.'

'How the hell are you going to find a missing person if you don't have their name?' asked Slater.

'There doesn't seem to be a description either,' said Watson, 'but there is a big doodle on the first page.'

'I can picture that,' said Slater. 'There's poor old Hudson telling Norton the love of his life is missing and Norton's doodling instead of listening.'

'Maybe he was working a long shift,' said Watson.

'Don't make excuses for him,' said Slater, testily.

'Sorry,' muttered Watson, 'but I'm not making excuses, I'm just saying.'

She turned another page and studied the crude shorthand. 'David Hudson obviously wasn't going to give up easily. Here's another entry dated 17 December. This time he's written the address again, and the name Howard Glossop.'

'Is there any mention of a visit to Glossop?' asked Slater. 'Only he said no one from the police ever contacted him.'

Watson was doing her best to read the unfamiliar shorthand as quick as she could. 'It doesn't look like it . . . Oh, hang on. Oh goodness, this is priceless,' she said, sarcastically. 'He's made a note that he believes the girl has left taking the baby with her. There's even another note underneath that, in longhand, that says, *I don't blame her.*'

'I bloody knew it,' said Slater, angrily. 'He didn't look for her at all, did he? Lazy bugger, he just didn't bother.' He turned and aimed an angry kick at the archive box, but it was a lot heavier than he had anticipated, and all he succeeded in doing was wrenching his ankle. 'Ow! Bollocks!' he said, sinking down into his own chair.

Watson continued with her head down, studying the notebook, until Slater had finished mumbling curses to himself. He had a sneaking suspicion she was trying to suppress a smirk.

'And let that be a lesson to you, Watson,' he said at last, swinging his chair round to face her. 'You should never kick an archive box, no matter how frustrated you might be feeling. They're heavier than they look.'

She swung her own chair round. 'Right, boss,' she said, acknowledging his rueful smile, 'I'll do my best to try to remember that. On a more serious note, what are we going to do about Norton?'

'What do you think we should do about him?'

'Well, I suppose we could point out to him how, if he had done his job properly, Kylie Mason might well have been found in 2000 and not nearly twenty years later.'

'That won't bring her back though, will it? Anyway, we're pretty much certain she was dead two months before Norton had even heard of her, or David Hudson. You have to ask yourself — did his actions actually stop her killer from being caught?'

'You're not suggesting we just ignore what he did, or rather what he *didn't* do, are you?'

'Certainly not,' said Slater, 'but I think we need to keep things in perspective. Norton deserves to have his arse kicked all over the place for the way he treated David Hudson, but right now, I am more concerned with solving two murders.'

'Yes, of course,' agreed Watson, 'so, what? Do we put him on the back burner for now?'

Slater pursed his lips. 'Before we do that, I think there's something we need to consider. I think we're both agreed Norton is pretty much a waste of space, right?'

Watson nodded her head. 'That's certainly the impression he gave me.'

'Okay then, bearing that in mind, should we just accept he didn't visit Glossop because he couldn't be bothered? Maybe, like you suggested, he was working long shifts in the run up to Christmas, and he was tired. Along comes David Hudson, claiming his girlfriend had gone missing with her baby. Norton goes to the cottage where Hudson claims they live, and when he gets there he finds someone else is living there who claims the place was empty when they moved in. There's no sign of a girl, or a baby, so he doesn't follow up with the landlord because he's decided this guy, Hudson, is some sort of nutter, and even if the girlfriend *does* exist, it's no wonder she's left him. He hasn't even written a report yet, and because he's tired, and he thinks it's all a waste of time, he doesn't even bother. Who can blame him?'

Watson looked at Slater in disbelief. 'You sound as if you almost feel sorry for him, and you're defending his behaviour!'

'Do I?'

'That's what it sounds like.'

'I'm just telling you what he wants us to believe,' said Slater. 'The thing is, I'm not sure we can trust Norton, and I do believe David Hudson. Plus, I also have a suspicious mind.'

'And what is your suspicious mind telling you?'

'It's telling me we should be asking this question: was Norton just too lazy to visit Howard Glossop and check Hudson's story? Or was there a reason he didn't check it? Glossop's office is only on the other side of the village. It's less than fifteen minutes from Ramlinstoke Police Station. It would have taken five minutes to check back through the previous tenants and confirm or deny Hudson's story.

It would have taken all of half an hour, and he would have known for sure.'

'Gosh,' said Watson. 'Are you suggesting he already knew what had happened to Kylie? I can see him being lazy and incompetent, but suggesting he's complicit in murder is a whole new ball game.'

'I'm not quite sure what I'm suggesting,' said Slater, 'but now the idea's in my head, I don't seem to be able to dismiss it.'

CHAPTER TWENTY-THREE

'I still can't figure out what might have happened to the baby,' said Watson later.

'You and me both,' agreed Slater.

'You don't think Kylie was killed for the baby, do you?'

'You mean someone wanted a baby that badly, they killed Kylie just to get their hands on hers?' asked Slater. 'So, if it was you, why would you pick on her?'

'She was a young mum, all on her own, just moved to a new house,' said Watson, who had clearly already given this some thought. 'Who's going to notice?'

Slater thought for a moment. 'Only her boyfriend,' he said. 'And we know that's the case because he was the only one who did actually notice.'

'That's right,' agreed Watson, 'but what if I knew he was away and would be away for another two months? By the time he gets back, I'm going to be long gone.'

Slater could see the logic, but he didn't feel convinced. 'So, you think someone picked Kylie out as being an easy target, knew David was away from home for a few weeks, and knew she was going to be moving to a new house where no one would know her? I think that would take a lot of planning, or one hell of a lot of luck, Sam. Maybe if it had happened in the last five years I might buy it, but that's a lot of information to gather, and don't forget you couldn't access information as easily back then as you can these days.'

'But the only alternative is someone coming across her at random, knocking her down, and taking the baby,' argued Watson. 'I don't find that any more likely. Most people would panic in that situation and run like hell. Anyway, if I suddenly appeared with a three-month-old baby, I'd have a lot of explaining to do, wouldn't I? It's not as if you can hide it away!'

Slater sighed. He shared her frustration. When you got down to it, they really were quite clueless about a lot of things in this case. 'We're missing something, somewhere,' he said, 'and my gut is telling me it's here, right in front of us, we're just not seeing it.'

'Do you want to go back to the beginning and start again?' she asked.

'We started with Diana and Alan Randall and that Irish pendant,' he said.

'You still think it's her son, don't you?' asked Watson. 'But how can it be if Hudson's the father? I thought we'd established there was no relationship between her and Hudson at the time Sonny was born.'

Slater heaved a heavy sigh. 'I know it doesn't add up,' he agreed, reluctantly. 'I just keep seeing her face when we showed her the photo of that pendant. She recognised it, I know she did.'

'Did you ever hear back from Mr Bradshaw about her?' asked Watson.

'Yes, I did,' said Slater.

'What about her resignation?'

'Apparently she left the job because she was suffering from depression,' said Slater.

'Was that after her son disappeared? I suppose that's fair enough. I should think that would be enough to depress anyone,' said Watson, gloomily.

Slater stopped. A little bell was ringing in his head. 'Where's your notebook?' he asked.

'Here on my desk, why?'

'Can you look up the notes from the day we went to the Randalls?'

She grabbed her notebook and began flipping through the pages until she found the right ones.

'I'm sure she told us she left fourteen years ago,' said Slater.

'Yes, you're right, she did,' confirmed Watson a few seconds later.

'But that was four years before her son went missing.'

'So that's not the reason she was depressed,' said Watson. 'Didn't Mr Bradshaw offer a reason why?'

'No,' said Slater. 'The only thing he had to offer was an unconfirmed rumour that she'd had an affair with another officer.'

'Did he think there was anything to it?' asked Watson.

'He gave me the name of a retired sergeant.' He checked the email again. 'Here it is, Ted Rivers. Apparently he used to be a desk sergeant.'

'He would probably know if there was any truth to the rumours,' said Watson. 'They tend to know everything.'

'Exactly,' agreed Slater. 'And I don't think Bradshaw would have given me his name just for the sake of it.'

'Well, there you are,' said Watson. 'If that's true, perhaps she was asked to leave or risk being exposed and face a scandal. They might have agreed she could use depression as an excuse.'

'Or maybe her husband found out and gave her an ultimatum,' Slater suggested. 'What if he told her she had to choose between the police or her family? Maybe the realisation she had messed her whole life up really did cause her to sink into depression.'

Slater dug around on his desk until he found their copy of the Flipton case file on Sonny Randall's disappearance. 'I'm going to take this back to the hotel tonight and have another look at the assessment of the parents. I'm sure it didn't mention anything about her suffering from depression at any time, but maybe I missed it.'

'I'm probably being dim,' said Watson, 'but even if she did have an affair, and she was, or wasn't, suffering from depression, I'm afraid I can't see how it's relevant to Kylie Mason's death, which was at least ten years earlier.'

'Oh, it isn't,' said Slater, 'but it might have something to do with her son's disappearance.'

'Right,' said Watson, 'I see.' But she didn't look or sound convinced.

Slater just hoped it wasn't going to be a monumental waste of his time.

CHAPTER TWENTY-FOUR

'So?' asked Watson the next morning. 'Did you learn anything from your homework last night?'

'I'm not sure,' said Slater, cagily. 'They did an assessment of both parents, as you would expect, but they both
came up squeaky clean.'

'That's not much help, is it?'

'I wouldn't be quite so quick to dismiss it,' warned Slater.
'It's not what it does say but what it doesn't that intrigues
me. According to what we've been told, she had only left her
job a couple of years earlier, citing depression as the reason
why. Now, that would have rung a few alarm bells if it was
my investigation, yet it doesn't even get a mention.'

'Just because someone suffers from depression, it doesn't
mean they killed their own son!'

'Of course it doesn't, but it should be of interest to the
investigation, yet it's not even mentioned.'

'Ah, yes, I see what you mean,' said Watson. 'Maybe
they thought it wasn't relevant.'

'It should still be in the file with a reason as to why it's
not relevant,' argued Slater.

'Well, yes, when you put it like that.'

'Right,' said Slater, 'so I started to wonder why it's not mentioned.'

'Investigating officers covering for her?' suggested Watson.

Slater pulled a face. 'I don't think so. Don't forget, this wasn't some minor fraud or something trivial. It was a missing kid, and in my opinion it looks like it was a pretty thorough investigation. I've got no reason to think anyone cut corners or covered anything up.'

'Okay, so why, then?' asked Watson.

'How about because it doesn't match anything in her actual health records.'

'Yes, but—'

'Her doctor's statement said she was fit and healthy, with no mention of any mental health issues.'

'But I thought she left her job because of depression.'

'That was the "official" version,' said Slater, waggling his fingers to create the inverted commas. 'We all know people who've left the force under a cloud, but there's nearly always an official version that paints a different story, isn't there? It's all about appearances rather than facts.'

'So this adds weight to your "illicit affair" theory, and I suppose now you want to pursue it?'

'It was Bradshaw's idea, not mine,' said Slater, 'but yes, it's got to be a possibility, and yes, I think we should look a bit deeper into it. There's definitely something fishy about her decision to leave the force. Whether it's actually relevant to our investigation remains to be seen.'

Watson smiled. 'In that case I think you'll be pleased with what I did last night.'

'You're not going to make me blush, are you, Sam?' he asked, with a wicked grin.

A few days ago she would have been flustered by Slater's comment and would have been blushing like a beetroot, but instead she just gave him a little smile. It was enough to tell him she was getting wise to him now and was beginning to take these comments, designed to embarrass, in her stride.

'I'm not sure I could, to be honest, boss,' she said, 'but I can promise you, if the chance ever comes along, I will take full advantage.'

Slater smiled his acknowledgement of the promise. 'Come, on then, I can't wait to hear your boudoir secrets.'

'Last night, I went looking for a man,' she said.

'And there I was, sitting on my bed, reading through a boring case file,' said Slater, tongue firmly in cheek. 'Did you find one?'

'Yes, I did. He's a bit old for me, but I think you'll like him. His name is Ted Rivers.'

'The retired sergeant?' asked Slater. 'You found him? But I didn't even ask—'

'It didn't look as if you were going to drop it, so I thought I might as well see if I could find him before you asked.'

'If this means another trip to Flipton, let's see if we can arrange to see everyone else involved in this case while we're up there, otherwise it's a whole day just to interview one person.'

Watson smiled a smile that told Slater she knew something he didn't know.

'What?' he asked, 'Why are you looking so pleased with yourself?'

'Why do you think he's in Flipton?'

'I just assumed if the guy was working up there he probably lives up there.'

'But he didn't work at Flipton,' said Watson, who looked like she was beginning to enjoy Slater's growing confusion.

'Well, how did he know she was having an affair with one of her colleagues at Flipton if he didn't work there?'

'Because he worked at Ramlinstoke.'

'What? But I thought . . .' Slater scratched his head. 'But she had left Ramlinstoke years before. Would an old, finished affair cost her her job?'

'That might depend on who she was having the affair with,' said Watson, 'but a couple of alternative possibilities came to mind. What if the affair had lapsed, but then the other officer had transferred to Flipton and it had started again? Or, what if it never ended and had carried on despite the distance involved? Maybe they used to meet halfway?'

'I dunno,' said Slater. 'I thought Flipton was the key, but now everything seems to be coming back to Ramlinstoke. I think we need to speak to your man. Can you give him a call?'

'I'll go and call him now.'

CHAPTER TWENTY-FIVE

At first, Ted Rivers seemed to be a little suspicious of Slater and Watson. He'd been retired for more than five years now, but it was evident he still felt the old resentment that was always stirred up when coppers started investigating each other.

'You're not these people who come round looking for someone to pin the blame on when things go wrong, are you?' he asked.

'If you mean Professional Standards, no we're not,' said Slater. 'At the moment we're looking into the death of a young woman and a child—'

'Are you the people over at Trillington?'

'Yes, that's right,' confirmed Slater. 'We look into old cases that were never solved. We don't specifically look for someone to blame, but I can't ignore it if I think someone hasn't even tried to do their job.'

'Got someone in mind, have you?' asked Rivers, suspiciously.

'How good's your memory?' asked Slater.

'I won't claim it's perfect, but it's not too bad. It depends on how obscure the case was.'

'In 2001, a guy called David Hudson was found guilty of assaulting DS Colin Norton.'

Rivers was smiling at the memory. 'Oh yes, I remember hearing all about that. Knocked Norton out cold with one punch. I was on leave at the time, but it was the talk of the station for weeks. I only wish I'd been there to see it.'

'Apparently there was a queue of well-wishers outside Hudson's cell, all waiting to shake his hand,' said Watson.

'That's what I heard,' said Rivers.

'Norton wasn't very popular, then?'

'About as well-liked as a swarm of wasps at a picnic.'

'Why was that?' asked Slater.

'Because he was a lazy, good-for-nothing slob,' said Rivers. 'He was a troublemaker too. Fancied himself as a ladies' man, and for some reason some of the ladies agreed with him.'

Watson wrinkled her nose.

'I see you've met him, then?' asked Rivers. 'Not your cup of tea?'

'Not if he was the last man on earth,' said Watson.

'Do you know why Hudson thumped him?' asked Slater.

'I wasn't involved in the case at all,' said Rivers. 'I heard the man had been brought in for being drunk and disorderly. I know Norton upset him somehow, but he had a knack for that. I'm just surprised more people didn't thump him.'

'Hudson had reported his girlfriend and baby missing,' said Slater, 'but Norton couldn't be bothered to do any proper police work to check it out. Instead, he decided Hudson was making it up, and told him he didn't blame the girl for running off and leaving him.'

Rivers shook his head. 'Like I said, bloody lazy, didn't care about people, or the job.'

'The thing is,' added Slater, 'we believe the young woman we've uncovered out at Trillington is David Hudson's girlfriend. She's been lying there for nearly twenty years.'

'So you really do have someone to blame this time,' said Rivers.

'He wouldn't have saved her life, but at least she could have been found,' said Slater. 'David Hudson's been wondering what happened for all that time.'

Rivers sighed. 'I never realised he was actually that lazy. My God, you wouldn't credit it would you? You can see why he's still a DS, although God only knows how he ever got that high up the ladder.'

There was a brief, gloomy silence, and then Slater spoke again. 'I was told you might be able to tell me about a young DS who worked at Ramlinstoke about twenty years ago. She went off to Flipton to become a DI.'

'D'you mean Diana Randall?' asked Rivers. 'Oh yes, I remember her. She got what you might call an assisted passage.'

Slater's ears pricked up. 'You mean she got special treatment? In exchange for what?'

Rivers' face lit up with a broad smile. 'Oh no, she wasn't bonking the chief constable if that's what you're thinking. When I say "assisted passage", I mean she came with a degree from some fancy university.'

'You mean she was fast-tracked through the system?'

'That's the word for it! Yes, she was fast-tracked. Personally, I don't think it's a good idea. I suppose a degree says something for a person, but it doesn't automatically make them a good detective, does it?'

'What was she like?'

'You just said it was twenty years ago,' said Rivers. 'I'm not sure I can remember.'

'Was she popular, like one of the lads? Or was she the studious type?'

'I seem to recall she would always be there in the pub after work buying her share of the rounds,' said Rivers. 'Like I said, she didn't need to study, she was fast-tracked. I don't think there's any substitute for experience and common sense, is there? And if my memory serves me right, that girl didn't have much of the latter.'

'Why's that?' asked Slater.

'Well, like I said, she wasn't bonking the chief constable . . .' He let the sentence trail away to silence.

'Yes, but?' insisted Slater.

Rivers looked uncomfortable. 'Why do you want to know all this stuff? It was years ago now.'

'Come on, Ted,' urged Slater. 'A good desk sergeant always has his finger on the pulse and knows what's going on, and that includes knowing who was seeing who. I can understand you're reluctant to point the finger at people, but this could be important.'

Rivers still seemed to be undecided.

'Look, nothing you tell us will be used,' Slater promised. He nodded across to Watson. 'Sam's not going to write any of this down, it's just background, but it might have some bearing on what happened.'

Rivers watched as Watson made a point of closing her notebook and putting it in her bag. This seemed to be enough to convince him.

'Well, it was nearly twenty years ago,' he said, 'and I suppose it won't hurt now, but if you tell anyone I told you, I shall deny it.'

Slater held up his hands. 'It was just a rumour we heard, right?'

Rivers nodded. 'Right, well, according to the rumour, Diana Randall was having it off with Colin Norton.'

Watson looked stunned, and Slater was having trouble picturing the immaculate Diana Randall with the uncouth slob that was Colin Norton. He kept his face impassive. 'And was there any foundation to the rumour?'

'You'd like to think any woman with an ounce of common sense would see him for what he was, but like I said, common sense was something she seemed to lack. I seem to recall her husband was older than her and was some sort of professor. He was clever and a bit refined, maybe she just fancied a bit of rough for a change.'

'Yes, but was the rumour true?' asked Slater, again.

'Well, I couldn't say for sure, because I never actually caught them red-handed,' said Rivers. 'But they did have a habit of "going off the air" when they were working together. It's amazing how often those two found areas where the radios didn't work, if you see what I mean? They wouldn't be gone for too long, but long enough, you know?'

'That's very helpful, Ted,' said Slater. 'I know it's not easy to tell us stuff like this.'

'It's not really that hard where an idiot like Norton's concerned.'

'Maybe, but I want you to know we really appreciate your help.'

Slater nodded to Watson to tell her it was time to go.

'Did Diana have any children?' asked Watson, as she got to her feet.

Rivers laughed. 'I don't think so. As I recall, she was always at work, busy being the career girl. A baby wouldn't have helped with that, now, would it?'

* * *

'I'm afraid I'm not sure I believe what we've just been told,' said Watson as she started Slater's car.

'What's that?' asked Slater.

'Oh, come on, Diana Randall and Colin Norton? How could she?'

'Ah,' said Slater, sagely. 'If there's one thing you should know by now, Sam, it's that there's no accounting for taste. When you look at Norton, you see an uncouth slob. Diana Randall sees Casanova.'

'No, I'm sorry,' she said. 'I just don't buy it. You've seen her, she keeps herself almost perfect, whereas he looks as if he doesn't care.'

'But it's carnal,' said Slater, warming to his subject. 'It's not about whether he's good-looking or not. Maybe he's some sort of sex machine and can keep going all night like that bunny in the advert for the fancy batteries.'

'Now that is just gross!' she said. 'Please, don't put an idea like that into my head, it's disgusting.'

'When I was a young lad,' said Slater, 'I was told you don't look at the mantelpiece when you're poking the fire! I guess it would work just as well for men and women.'

'Sorry?' said Watson. 'I'm not with you.'

Slater was beginning to feel somewhat awkward and regretting allowing his mouth to run away with him. This conversation was in danger of backfiring if he wasn't careful. 'Err, well, I suppose if I'm honest, it was a sort of bloke thing,' he admitted, 'from years back. It was what the older guys used to say to try to impress the youngsters like me.'

Watson gave him a swift glance. 'And do you?' she asked, focusing back on the road ahead as she drove.

Slater swivelled his head to look at her. 'Do I what?' He could see the beginnings of a smile on her face.

'Look at the mantelpiece when you're poking the fire?'

Slater was big enough to admit he'd brought this on himself, and he was quietly pleased Watson was prepared to play the game and seize the chance to get her own back. He thought for a moment before he spoke.

'We have gas central heating,' he said, with a grin, 'and anyway, I always turn the lights off.'

Watson's smile widened, but she didn't say anything.

'Getting back to Diana Randall, don't they say opposites attract?' asked Slater.

'They don't attract me.'

'Fair comment,' said Slater. 'But her husband's older, right? Ted Rivers said he was a bit refined. Maybe she was bored.'

'Alright,' said Watson. 'Let's say it is true, and they were having an affair. How does it help our case?'

'I don't know,' said Slater. 'But there's got to be some connection between Diana Randall, Colin Norton and David Hudson. There are just too many coincidences for my liking. What if Hudson was the father of Diana's baby? And then while he's away, Norton moves onto the scene and starts an affair with her. Hudson comes back, finds out, and punches Norton's lights out? Maybe Hudson then moved up to Flipton because he wanted to rekindle his affair with her.'

'That's very good, sir,' said Watson, 'but what about Kylie Mason and her baby?'

'Maybe he was cheating on her,' Slater suggested.

'That gives him an even better motive for killing her,' agreed Watson, 'but don't forget he still has the Kosovo alibi.'

Slater studied the road ahead for a few moments. 'No, you're right,' he said. 'It doesn't work, does it?'

'Only if he wasn't in Kosovo,' she said, as she stopped the car and switched off the engine, 'and we know he was.'

CHAPTER TWENTY-SIX

'Even I'm impressed with the speed of the guys at the lab,' said Cutter.

Slater and Watson had returned to find a pinned note on the door asking them to come to the MAFU truck right away. 'And?' said Slater impatiently.

'As a result of their work, I can inform you the initial findings from the DNA samples we sent from our latest victim suggests she is the mother of our first victim.'

Slater looked confused. 'But Kylie's child was a baby.'

'I'm only saying we have the skeletons of a mother and her son,' said Cutter, 'and I must stress, these are preliminary results and have to be confirmed.'

'So, if we know the boy is Hudson's son, can we say for sure that this is Kylie Mason?' asked Slater.

'We can say it's likely, but there's always the possibility Hudson had this child with another woman, and the body we have is the other woman. The only way we can prove this is Kylie is if you can get a DNA sample from the parents, then we could prove it beyond doubt.'

'Right,' said Slater, turning to Watson. 'That's got to be our next call.'

Watson absently nodded her agreement. It looked like something was bothering her. She looked at Cutter, who smiled at her. 'Can I ask a question?'

'Of course.'

'Didn't you tell us this young woman was around eighteen?'

'That's right,' he said, encouragingly. 'We estimate the young woman to have been around eighteen to twenty years old when she died and, as you know, the child was somewhere between five and ten.'

He stopped speaking and looked expectantly at her face. It took a few seconds for the penny to drop.

'Goodness!' said Watson. 'That means the mother was just a child herself. She couldn't have been more than thirteen when she gave birth!'

'Or possibly even younger, if you're following that train of thought,' added Cutter.

'Jesus!' said Slater. 'If that's right, this can't be Kylie! Are you sure about their ages?'

'We were lucky to have two full sets of teeth as well as the bones. It's true we can't tell you their exact ages yet, but I would stake my reputation on our estimates. I've asked for much more detailed analysis, to be more accurate, but that will take a few days.'

Watson and Slater exchanged a look.

'But hang on a minute, this doesn't make sense,' said Slater. 'When we went to see David Hudson, the boy's father, he showed us photos of the mother. He says she was eighteen when the kid was born, and the photos back that up.'

'And I'm sure that's probably correct,' said Cutter.

'Well, make your mind up,' said Slater, testily. 'You just told us the mother was a child.'

'No,' said Cutter. 'I didn't say that. You two jumped to that conclusion, but there is another possible explanation. I would suggest it could also mean the mother was killed some time ago and the child was kept somewhere for several years before he, too, was killed, and then buried close to his mother.'

'But didn't you say the boy couldn't be more than ten years old, and might be as young as five?' asked Watson.

'That's right.'

'So, if he has been kept somewhere, it's possible he had only just been born when the mother died?'

'It has to be a possibility, yes,' agreed Cutter.

'So this could still be Kylie,' said Slater. 'Could she have died in childbirth?'

'The state of the skeletal pelvis suggests she had given birth not long before her death, but the pelvis is damaged, so it's almost impossible to say how recently with any certainty.'

'But it's a possibility?' persisted Slater.

'I'd say it's a possibility, but unlikely,' conceded Cutter.

'Okay, Henry,' said Slater. 'This is what we think we've got so far. Eighteen-year-old Kylie Mason had a baby in July 2000 while her husband-to-be, David Hudson, was in Kosovo. On 20 October she moved into Trillington while Hudson was still away. The baby doesn't sleep well, and she had taken to walking the streets carrying the kid to get him to sleep. The watch you found suggests she died at 22.45 on 22 October. That ties in with our story, because she disappeared around then. Would this scenario fit with what you have found?'

'Get me that DNA sample from her parents and we'll know for sure it's her,' said Cutter, 'but yes, it all seems to add up, doesn't it?'

'All except the baby,' said Watson.

'Yes, that's the million-dollar question,' muttered Slater. 'What happened to the baby? Where was he for all that time? And how did he come to end up alongside his mother, years later?'

CHAPTER TWENTY-SEVEN

Number fifteen Maple Avenue was a small bungalow typical
of so many others built in the seventies in the small seaside
town of Inglethorpe on the south coast. Just like its neighbours, it had been modernised with double-glazed windows,
a new front door, a small extension on one side, and a con-
servatory on the other side to catch the evening sun. The
immaculate garden was a tribute to a green-fingered resident
and was in perfect keeping with all the others in the avenue.
As he climbed from the car, Slater felt optimistic, and as
he followed Watson to the front door, he reflected on how
funny it was that one's surroundings could do that.

She rang the doorbell and they waited. 'Nice garden,'
she observed.

Slater took a closer look at his surroundings. He wasn't
what you might call a keen gardener; reluctant would have
been a much more fitting adjective. It was all he could do to
mow his small patch of grass when he remembered, but he
had to agree being in this garden did make him feel good.
He remembered he had read somewhere that gardening was
supposed to be therapeutic and good for the soul. Maybe he
should think about taking it up — he often felt he could do
with a hobby. His thoughts were interrupted by the sound

of the front door opening and he turned his attention back to the job in hand, and to the bright-eyed, silver-haired lady smiling at them.

'Mrs Mason?' asked Watson.

'Pardon?' She was obviously hard of hearing. 'If you're Jehovah's Witnesses, we're not interested.'

Watson opened her wallet and showed her warrant card. 'We're from the police,' she announced. 'I'm DS Brearley, and this is DI Slater.'

Mrs Mason peered uncertainly at the unfamiliar couple on her doorstep and then looked at the warrant card. 'Police?' she said. 'We didn't call for the police.'

'No, you didn't,' agreed Watson, 'but we'd like to talk to you if you don't mind.'

Mrs Mason leaned out of the door and looked up and down the road, apparently concerned what the neighbours might think. 'Am I under arrest?' she asked conspiratorially. 'I'll come quietly, there's no need for the neighbours to know.' Her voice had faded as she uttered the last sentence, soundlessly mouthing the last few words.

Slater was trying hard not to smile, but he had not seen Watson looking flustered before and was finding her obvious discomfort quite hard to resist. He was wondering exactly how Watson was going to deal with the situation, especially when Mrs Mason offered her wrists towards her with the words, 'Okay, cuff me if you must.' Now he had to turn away.

Mrs Mason was obviously quite harmless, but it was equally obvious she had no idea what was going on. Talking to her was going to be hard work, and it seemed unlikely they would get any sense out of her. Slater was enjoying the situation so much he had turned away to have a good laugh at Watson's expense.

'No, Mrs Mason,' she said, carefully enunciating every syllable. 'We need to come inside and speak to you.'

'Inside? Shouldn't I face trial first? You haven't even told me what I've done?'

'It's about your daughter,' explained Watson, slowly, and now, for the first time, Mrs Mason seemed to join them in the real world, but before she could speak, a man appeared at the door behind her. He gently placed his hands on her shoulders.

'We don't have a daughter,' he said. 'We haven't had one for years.'

'Are you Mr Mason?' asked Watson.

The man was in his seventies, but he stood tall and proudly defiant. 'I am,' he said, sternly, 'and I'd appreciate it if you would go away and stop bothering my wife. You can see she's not well.'

'Mr Mason, we wouldn't be here if this wasn't important. It's about your daughter, Kylie.'

At the mention of Kylie's name, his wife looked round at him, eyes pleading.

'I told you, we don't have a daughter,' said Mr Mason.

'Your wife seems to think you have,' said Watson, and Mrs Mason looked back at her, bright eyes now filled with tears. 'And those tears look real enough.'

Mason drew his wife into his arms. 'I don't want her getting upset.'

'I'm afraid I can't promise that,' said Watson. 'Can we come inside, please?'

'We haven't set eyes on the little bitch in nearly twenty years,' he said, bitterly. 'It's her fault her mother's like this. If she had wanted to see us, she knew where we were, no one was stopping her. Now you're just causing her more upset.'

Watson looked into Mrs Mason's frightened eyes, and then up at her husband again. 'I don't think it's me that's upsetting your wife, Mr Mason. Please let us in. The sooner we come in, the sooner we'll go away and leave your wife in peace.'

Mason seemed to be fighting his own indecision, but eventually he relented. 'I want you to understand I'm not happy about this,' he said.

'That's duly noted, Mr Mason,' said Watson, 'but I promise you, we wouldn't be here if it wasn't important.'

Mason led them into a neat and tidy sitting room. He pointed to the two armchairs, and then, keeping hold of his wife's hand, he led her across to the settee where the two of them sat, hand in hand.

'I suppose she's in some sort of trouble, is she?' asked Mason. 'I always knew it would happen, sooner or later. I told her to keep away from that man, but she wouldn't listen. Got herself banged up by him and then cleared off. We never heard a word from her, you know? Honestly, you bring them up as best you can, and then the ungrateful little buggers just up and leave.'

Watson waited for him to run out of steam, before she spoke. 'Actually,' she said, 'the story we heard wasn't quite like that. We heard you asked her to leave when she got pregnant. You told her she had to choose between you and David Hudson.'

Mason's wife tried to draw her hand away from him, and he looked momentarily furious. 'Now look what you've done,' he snapped. 'How dare you come here spreading lies like that!'

'I'll ask you to keep your temper under control, Mr Mason,' said Slater. 'Judging from the look on your wife's face, she's just heard the truth for the first time in many years.'

'That daughter of ours broke her heart,' said Mason. 'I kept telling her to stay away from that Hudson character. I tried everything to keep them apart. You would have done, too. And what happened? He got her pregnant. I knew he was a bad sort. I expect she never saw him again after that.'

'So you kicked her out when she was pregnant,' said Watson, 'and you didn't have a clue what happened to her?'

'Don't you judge me, young lady. It's that Hudson you need to judge, not me.'

'David Hudson was the one who looked out for her,' argued Watson. 'He was the one who found her a flat to live in. He was the one who helped her pay the rent. He was the one who left the army to look after her and their son. He was the one who found them a cottage to live in after the baby was born.'

Mason looked suitably uncomfortable.

'So you had no idea you had a grandson?'

Mason just shook his head. Mrs Mason may have been unwell, but she was well enough to understand what was going on. 'Where is she?' she wailed.

'There's no easy way to say this,' said Watson, 'but I'm afraid we believe she is dead, Mrs Mason. I'm sorry.'

The scream was both unexpected and chilling. It obviously completely unnerved Watson, and Slater, too, felt he'd never heard anything quite like it before. Mr Mason grabbed his wife and clutched her to his chest. At first she tried to fight him off, beating him with her fists, but eventually she gave up and let him pacify her.

'Did you have to do this?' asked Mason. The fight seemed to have drained out of him now.

'I'm afraid we have a duty to identify the body,' said Slater, 'and we have a duty to notify the next of kin.'

'And are you sure it's her?'

'Ninety per cent sure,' said Slater. 'DNA samples from the two of you will confirm it.'

'Of course. Just give my wife a minute or two.'

'Yes, take your time,' said Slater. 'We don't want to make this any worse than it is.'

'When did it happen?'

'We believe she died in October 2000,' explained Watson.

'How?'

'We don't know for sure yet.'

'You mean she was killed?'

Watson didn't answer.

'Well, I'd look very closely at that David Hudson,' said Mason. 'He'd be my prime suspect.'

'I hate to disappoint you,' said Slater, 'but David Hudson was in Kosovo on his last tour of duty before he left the army to spend his life with Kylie. It was only when he returned that anyone even knew she was missing.'

'She was on her own, you see. He was all she had,' added Watson. 'He says he tried to get in touch with you several times.'

'I had no time for the man,' said Mason.

'Yes, you've made that quite clear,' said Watson. There was so much more she wanted to add, but she wouldn't, not in front of Mrs Mason.

CHAPTER TWENTY-EIGHT

'Hello, Slater, it's DCI Lipton here. I just called to see how your visit to the Randalls went.'

'Hello, sir, I suspect you already know how it went, and now you're calling to give me the bollocking you warned me about,' Slater said. 'I'm surprised it's taken you so long to call.'

Lipton laughed. 'Alan Randall only called me yesterday. Apparently Diana was very upset when you left.'

'I wasn't exactly happy,' said Slater. 'It took us more than three hours to get there, and then we were only there about five minutes and he asked us to leave.'

'Was that when you asked about a DNA sample? I thought that might happen.'

'You could have warned me,' said Slater. 'We wasted the best part of day driving all the way up there and then back.'

'Well, now you see what you're up against,' said Lipton. 'They wouldn't give us a sample either. Diana insisted they would only do it if we found her son.'

'Didn't you think that was strange?' asked Slater.

'Of course, but what can you do? She started on about data protection and all that crap.'

'Anyway, it doesn't matter now, we've got DNA evidence to prove it's not their son,' said Slater.

'Well, I'll be damned!' said Lipton. 'What about the pendant?'

'You've got me there,' admitted Slater, 'I'm certain Diana recognised the pendant when I showed it to her, but she's adamant it's not her son's, and at the moment I can't prove any different. Besides, they tell me DNA doesn't lie.'

'You sound disappointed.'

'I am. It was the way she reacted to the pendant. I was convinced it was their son.'

'Are you going to go back and apologise?' asked Lipton.

'Is that what you want me to do?'

'He's insisting you should, but I wouldn't blame you if you didn't.'

Slater was thinking. 'D'you know, I think that might be a good idea. I'm sure the Randalls are hiding something, maybe I can find out what it is. I'll tell them you sent me to apologise.'

'I'll expect another call from them, shall I?' asked Lipton.

'I'll do my best not to upset anyone, but I can't promise.'

'You know, Slater, I get the impression you're not the sort who loses sleep over the idea of upsetting people in pursuit of an inquiry.'

'I have to admit, the Randalls aren't the first people I've upset,' confessed Slater.

Lipton laughed. 'A man after my own heart. I thought as much. Is there anything we can do to help from this end?'

'Well, it's quite possible there is,' said Slater. 'Let me explain what's going on . . .'

* * *

As Slater put the phone down, he felt DCI Lipton had just done him a big favour by giving him an excuse to revisit the Randalls, and he was determined to make sure he made the most of it.

The revelation that Kylie Mason was the mother of the little boy certainly seemed to have eliminated the possibility of the child being Sonny Randall, but he was still convinced they were missing something, even if it wasn't related to their inquiry, so he decided he would have to go back through Diana Randall's work history again. He wasn't sure what he was hoping to find, but now he knew about her relationship with Colin Norton, maybe he would spot something he had previously dismissed as not being relevant.

CHAPTER TWENTY-NINE

If Diana Randall was surprised to see them when she swung her front door open, she certainly managed to hide it, but she made no attempt to hide the distasteful curl of her lip. Slater gave her a cheery smile. Being unpopular didn't bother him one little bit, and he was happy to know he was already getting under her skin.

'Good morning Mrs Randall,' he said. 'DCI Lipton was most insistent we should come back and see you.'

'What do you want?' she snapped.

'If we could just come inside for a couple of minutes. DCI Lipton felt we owed you an apology.'

For a moment it looked as though she was considering slamming the door in their faces, but then she relented and stepped back inside. 'I suppose you'd better come in,' she said, sullenly.

They followed her inside, Watson carefully closing the door behind them.

'Is Mr Randall here?' asked Slater. 'We seemed to upset both of you last time we were here, so it's only right we should apologise to both of you.'

'I'm afraid my husband's away on business. He won't be back until tomorrow morning.'

'Oh dear, what a pity,' said Slater.

'I'll pass your apologies on,' said Diana.

'While we're here, I'd like to ask one or two questions if that's okay?'

'I don't see how you can have any questions I can possibly help you with,' said Diana, testily. 'I've already told you it's not my son you've found!'

'Oh, we know it's not your son, Mrs Randall,' said Watson. 'We have DNA evidence to show his father was a man called David Hudson. I don't suppose you know him?'

Diana seemed to be completely nonplussed by Watson's question. Her mouth flapped open a couple of times before she gathered her thoughts and actually spoke. 'That's a coincidence,' she said. 'There used to be a David Hudson living on the farm next door, but it can't be the same man, can it?'

'Did you know him before he came to live on the farm?' asked Slater.

'What? Why would I have known him?'

'I just wondered,' said Slater. 'You see, he rented a cottage in Trillington. You know Trillington, don't you?'

'Of course I do, it's not far from Ramlinstoke where I used to work.'

'But you never met Mr Hudson while you were there?'

'No, I did not! Are you trying to suggest I'm somehow connected to this dead child through him?'

'Good heavens, no,' said Slater. 'The DNA results also told us who the mother of the child is — or was. Her name was Kylie Mason.'

Diana had gone extremely pale all of a sudden. 'Excuse me,' she said, and holding her hand to her mouth, she rushed from the room, across the hall, and into a small downstairs cloakroom. She slammed the door behind her. The sounds of retching could clearly be heard. It was a good five minutes before Diana emerged, her face still deathly pale.

'I'm sorry,' she explained. 'It must be something I ate.'

'There's lot of it around,' said Slater. 'Let's hope it's nothing serious.'

'I'm sure I'll be fine once I've had a lie down,' she said.

'Yes, of course,' said Slater. 'We'll get out of your way and let you recover. There's just one more thing before we go. Do you know a DS Colin Norton?'

'Yes. We were colleagues at Ramlinstoke.'

'Good friends, were you?'

'No, I didn't really know him that well. Like I said, we were colleagues, nothing more, nothing less.'

'Oh, I thought you must have been good friends,' said Slater. 'Didn't he take some leave and come up here to help with the search for your son when he went missing?'

Diana licked her lips nervously. 'Well, yes, he did, but I don't know why. Perhaps he was at a loose end and wanted to do something useful,' she said, unconvincingly.

Slater stared at her, making it quite clear what he thought of her lies without actually saying as much.

'Here's another coincidence for you, Mrs Randall,' said Watson. 'Kylie Mason, the child's mother, was found in the same ditch as her son.'

'You found him in a ditch?' Diana sounded horrified.

'Oh, I'm sorry, didn't we mention that before? He was found in a ditch, just along from his mother. It looks like she was killed by a hit-and-run driver and was either knocked into the ditch or dumped in there.'

Slater and Watson stared at Diana Randall, waiting for some sort of response. 'I really think I need to go and lie down,' she said, putting a hand to her head.

'Yes, I think that's probably a good idea,' said Slater. 'We'll see ourselves out.'

CHAPTER THIRTY

Slater climbed into the driver's seat, clicked his seat belt on, and started the car. 'So what did you make of that?' he asked, as he pulled away.

'Did you tell her we were coming?' asked Watson.

'No, I didn't, but she was definitely expecting us, wasn't she?'

'She complained to DCI Lipton, didn't she?' asked Watson. 'Would he have told her?'

'I couldn't honestly say for sure,' said Slater, thoughtfully, 'but I don't think he has any more time for the Randalls than you or I have.'

'Ted Rivers?' asked Watson.

'I got the impression he didn't much care for her,' said Slater.

'That rather narrows the field then, doesn't it?' asked Watson.

Slater quickly aimed a smile in her direction. 'So you spotted the bullshit about not really knowing Colin Norton?'

'She really must think we're all stupid,' said Watson. 'He wouldn't even have known her son had disappeared if he wasn't in touch with her.'

'He might have seen it on the daily bulletin,' said Slater.

'Yes, he might have seen it a couple of days after the event, but we know he was there the very next morning, his name's on the search list! Do you want me to get hold of his phone records?'

'There you go again, thinking the same thing as me and planning ahead,' said Slater. 'It's beginning to look like I have the perfect partner. I like that.'

Watson blushed at the compliment, and they drove on in silence for a minute or two.

'What about her reaction when you mentioned the ditch?' asked Slater.

'It is quite a horrific idea when you think about it,' said Watson. 'Some poor kid dumped in a cold, wet ditch all alone.' She gave an involuntary shiver.

'Yeah, I suppose it could have been that,' said Slater.

'But you don't think it was?'

'I'm beginning to feel we may have missed something by not pursuing it, but perhaps it's just me and I'm seeing things that aren't there.'

'You mean your dislike of her is stopping you from being objective?'

'Yeah, I suppose,' agreed Slater, reluctantly. 'If it's that obvious, it's not very professional, is it?'

'Some people are very easy to dislike, and she's certainly one of them,' said Watson. 'But, don't worry, I'll say if I think you're too far out of line.'

Slater inclined his head in acceptance, but said nothing.

'What if she's right about what she said the first time we spoke to her, and the St Christopher pendant was taken from their son and given to the dead boy?' asked Watson.

'If that's the case, we've still got another body to find,' said Slater, 'but, quite honestly, I'd prefer it if we could make do with the two bodies we already have.'

'Of course, if it's the same person behind the abductions, it's possible that Sonny Randall might still be alive.'

Slater took his eyes off the road to glance in Watson's direction. 'How do you work that one out?'

'Suppose the whole idea was to steal a little boy and then turn him into some sort of slave?'

'You mean for sex?' asked Slater.

Watson pulled a face. 'Well, yes, I suppose so.'

'God, I hope not,' said Slater. 'Anyway, why have two?'

'Perhaps it was always intended there would only be one, but it went wrong and he died.'

'What, and then he steals the Randalls' son as a replacement?' asked an incredulous Slater.

'It's possible,' said Watson.

Slater looked across at Watson again, and then turned back to the road. 'I had you down as an innocent, maybe even a bit naive, but I can see I was wrong. I thought you hadn't dealt with this sort of thing before?'

'I only said I'd never had to deal with a missing child, but I've worked a bit of Vice before.'

'So, there's a whole lot more to Samantha Brearley than meets the eye,' said Slater with a mischievous grin.

'Never judge a book by its cover,' said Watson, with a twinkle in her eye. 'You should know that, sir.'

They drove on in silence for a couple of minutes before Slater spoke again. 'If you're just gazing out of the window, do you think you could take another look through the Diana Randall file? I've studied it and studied it, but I'm sure I've missed something. It's on the back seat.'

CHAPTER THIRTY-ONE

Watson raised her eyebrows, but then reached back for the file. 'I know you're the boss, but can I ask why you're so focused on Diana Randall?'

'You mean, is there more to it than the fact I don't like her?'

'Well, I accept we're pretty sure she is, or at least was, up to something with Colin Norton, but as far as we know it was just an affair, and that's not actually a crime, is it? I know you've asked me to go through the file because you think you're missing something, but as we know her son's not one of our victims, I can't see how it's relevant to our investigation.'

'Do you think I have some sort of vendetta against her?' asked Slater.

'I wouldn't put it quite like that,' she said, diplomatically, 'but we're not giving David Hudson this much attention.'

'That's because we know he has an alibi for the time Kylie died,' said Slater.

'When did Diana become a suspect in Kylie's murder?'

'As we don't have anything to go on right now, every-one's a suspect in Kylie's murder,' said Slater.

'I hope you're not proposing that for real.'

'What? No, of course not,' said Slater. 'Look, I can't tell you what exactly it is I suspect Diana Randall of doing, and maybe I'm completely wrong, I'm just convinced she's done something.'

'It's because of that pendant, isn't it?'

'You were there, Sam. You saw her face. It was the same when you told her about the ditch. It meant something significant to her.'

Watson nodded slowly. 'But what if she was right and it was just a similar pendant, or someone had taken it from her son and given it to Kylie's son? What if she had met David Hudson and given it to him, and then he'd given it to his son?'

'You're clutching at straws there and you know it,' said Slater. 'I mean, what are the chances? David Hudson had never met his son, and I can't even see how Diana could have met Hudson, and anyway we've already ruled him out as a figure of interest.'

Watson sighed. 'I suppose you're right about Hudson. I think he stopped being a figure of interest when you asked him if he was the father of Diana Randall's son, and he nearly had a coronary at the very idea.'

'I didn't put it quite as bluntly as that,' said Slater.

'Well, no, but you have to admit he did look pretty horrified at the idea. Poor man, he didn't even get to share the experience of seeing his son born or get the chance to take some time off to enjoy his first few days.'

An alarm bell was suddenly ringing in Slater's head. What had she just said? 'Can you say that again?'

'The bit where he was horrified?'

'No, what came after that.'

'I said he didn't even get the chance to take a few days off to be with the baby.'

'That's it! How could I be so stupid? I told you I'd missed something, didn't I?'

There was a lay-by just ahead, and he quickly indicated and pulled over into it. He reached a hand towards her. 'Can I have that file back a minute?'

'What is it?' asked Watson, passing him the file.

'You just said it,' he said, flipping through the file. 'When we spoke to Hudson he was really indignant I should even suggest he was the father of Diana's son, right? But he went further, didn't he? He told us the boy had been born before the major took him up to Flipton Dene, and that was before he met Diana.'

'Right,' said Watson, uncertainly. She really wasn't sure where Slater was headed with this.

'Think about the dates. The major took Hudson up there when he came out of prison, so it was the latter half of 2001. We know Diana was a DI at Flipton by then, and she would never have got that promotion if she had been pregnant.'

'So, the baby must have been born while she was still at Ramlinstoke,' said Watson, matter-of-factly, 'before she became a DI. I don't see why that's a problem.'

'No?' asked Slater. 'Well, let me explain. The Randalls claimed Sonny was six years old when he disappeared. That means he must have been born in 2000, right?'

'Yes, and?' asked Watson.

'Don't you see?' asked Slater. 'That was the year Diana got her promotion.'

'And that worries you because?'

'That worries me because I don't believe they would have promoted someone that young who had just had a baby.'

'That's a bit sexist, isn't it?' asked Watson, derisively. 'Do you really think they would penalise her for having a baby?'

'Come on, get real,' said Slater. 'Of course they would, but that's not what I'm getting at.' He finally found the page he had been looking for and passed it across to Watson. 'Here you are. There's no mention anywhere in this file of her ever having taken maternity leave. I mean, whoever heard of a woman having a baby and going straight back to work?'

'She's a career girl,' said Watson. 'Maybe her husband looked after the baby and she cut her maternity leave short.'

'But according to her records, she's never had more than the odd day off sick. Now, I'll admit I don't know much about childbirth, but she would have to be superwoman to be back at work the next day, wouldn't she?'

Watson stared at him for a long moment. 'Perhaps they adopted,' she said. 'I'll get the team to check.'

'Tell them to get a move on,' said Slater. 'We're going back up there tomorrow and I want some answers before we get there.'

'Do you want to go back now?'

'I don't think so,' said Slater. 'I want Alan to be there. They knew we were coming today. Next time, I want to surprise them.'

* * *

That evening, just after eight, Slater's phone began to ring.

'Hi, Norm, what do you know?'

'I went round to your flat on my walk this morning, like you asked, and I knocked on the door, but there was no answer. I looked through the windows but, if I'm honest, I would have to say the place looks empty. I'm pretty sure Jenny's not there.'

'Oh, right,' said Slater, gloomily. 'Well, thanks for going round there, mate.'

'That's okay,' said Norman. 'These walks can get pretty boring, so it gave me a change of scenery. Look, is there something I should know?'

'She's pissed off about me working away,' explained Slater. 'Every time we've spoken since I got here, all she's done is complain about being left on her own. Then the last couple of nights she's not even answered my calls.'

'Ah, right, I see,' said Norman. 'So you think what?'

'Well, I thought she was just trying to annoy me by ignoring me, but if she's not there, well, I dunno what to think, really.'

'She hasn't left you, has she?' asked Norman, bluntly.

'Good grief, no,' said Slater, a little too hastily. 'She said something about going to her parents to try and make the peace. I expect that's where she is.'

'Do you want me to get my spare key and go round and take a look?'

'What? No, I don't think so, Norm. I'll admit I was a bit worried, but I wouldn't want her to think we were spying on her.'

'It's no trouble—'

'No, it's okay, Norm. There's no need for you get involved in one of our domestics. You know how Jenny likes to make a big deal out of these things. She's always threatening to leave me, but she never does. I'm sure we'll be fine once I get back. It will all blow over, you'll see.'

'Okay, but if you change your mind, just let me know?'

'Sure I will, thanks Norm.'

Slater ended the call and tossed his phone onto the bed. This was worse than he had thought. Maybe this time, she really had packed her bags and gone!

CHAPTER THIRTY-TWO

It was a pretty quiet journey up to Flipton Dene the next morning. Slater wasn't in the mood for talking, and thankfully Watson seemed to realise that and stayed quiet too. About an hour from the Randalls', her mobile phone began to ring.

Slater was deep in thought and barely heard Watson's conversation. He hadn't heard from Jenny since the night before last, and it was beginning to worry him. This was the first time they had been apart since they had started living together, but they had been in an ongoing argument for the first few days about her being on her own. Even so, he had been quite sure she was okay. Then she had told him she was going to see her parents to try to make the peace.

Of course, he had been pleased to think she was finally going to start putting her life back together, but why hadn't she called him back last night? He thought maybe it was because she was with her parents and hadn't seen them in a long time, and there was lots of catching up to do, but even as he tried to convince himself, he knew he was making a pretty lame excuse for her. She knew he worried about her, but she always told him she was fine and he shouldn't fuss.

He had called her twice and left a message each time. She should have called back, but she hadn't even sent a text. He wondered if she sulking again, or was this some perverse idea of hers to teach him he shouldn't worry? If it was, it was having totally the opposite effect. His gloomy thoughts were interrupted when he became aware Watson was speaking to him.

'Sir?'

He glanced across at her, almost surprised to see her there. 'I'm sorry, I was miles away.'

'You have been ever since we left this morning.'

'Yeah, I'm sorry about that,' he said, sheepishly. 'I should leave personal stuff at home.'

'But sometimes that's easier said than done, isn't it?' said Watson. 'Especially when you've got the best part of three hours on the motorway in front of you. Remember you told me I shouldn't be afraid to show I'm human? Well, that goes for you, too. I wouldn't want a robot for a boss any more than you want one for a partner.'

Slater thought that was fair enough and conceded the point without comment. 'Well, anyway, I'm here now,' he said. 'What did you want?'

She waggled her phone at him. 'That was the team. I told them you wanted some quick results, and they've got some. It turns out Diana Randall has a maternal great-grandmother who was Irish. A devout Catholic, she lived in Dublin before she came over to England. That doesn't prove there's a link between her and the silversmith who made the pendant, but it lends a bit more credence to the theory.'

'So maybe great-granny was given the pendant as a child and then it passes down through the girls in the family,' said Slater.

'Until it gets to Diana, and she doesn't have a daughter so she gives it to her son,' finished Watson.

'It works as a theory,' said Slater, 'but it's just circumstantial at best if we can't prove it.'

'There's more,' said Watson. 'It appears the Randalls have never adopted a child. At least, not officially.'

Slater whistled appreciatively. 'Now, that is interesting,' he said, with a broad grin. 'That has definitely brightened my day. Well done, Sam!'

148

'I thought you'd like that,' said Watson, looking pleased to have lightened his mood, 'but I can't claim the credit, it's the team, not me.'

'Oh yes, I like that very much,' purred Slater, happily. He had to admit he was very impressed with 'the team', as Watson called them, but he was feeling rather guilty that he had no idea who these people were, and he had never met, or even spoken to, a single one of them.

'So tell me about this team back at base. What's the story behind them?'

'They're what Mr Bradshaw calls his secret weapon,' explained Watson.

'What does he mean by that?'

'Well, they're not exactly what you might expect.'

'In what way?'

'They're mostly civilians, not police officers.'

'Civilians are being used more and more as backroom staff,' said Slater, 'so what makes this lot so special?'

'They're not what you'd call your average civilian. They've all got high security clearance, and they've all been rescued from the scrapheap by Mr Bradshaw, a bit like me.'

'You need to stop talking about yourself like that,' said Slater. 'You were never going to end up on anyone's scrapheap, you're far too bright for that to happen.'

'It's very nice of you to say so, but I was going to be put out to grass,' she said, 'there's no getting away from that. And then along came Mr Bradshaw. He keeps a list of names, all people from the military or police, all of whom have been forced to give up active roles through injury. The way he sees it, the fact that someone is no longer fully able-bodied doesn't mean they can no longer think. He believes a good brain should be used, not discarded.'

'I suddenly see him in a new light,' said Slater, somewhat taken aback by this news. 'I knew he'd rescued your career, but I had no idea he was doing it on a grand scale.'

'It's not a problem for you, is it?'

'Are you kidding? I think he's got it exactly right, and they've certainly convinced me they know what they're doing. I want you to make sure you take me to meet them all once we get the chance. I owe someone a bottle of champagne. Shanaya, wasn't it? I'd like to deliver it in person.'

'I'm sure she would like that very much,' said Watson. 'I'll do my best to arrange something once we've solved this case.'

'That's a date then,' said Slater. 'Now let's go and see what the Randalls have to say for themselves this morning.'

CHAPTER THIRTY-THREE

Alan Randall looked like a man who hadn't slept in days when he opened the door to them. 'What have you done?' he demanded as soon as he set eyes on Slater.

'I'm sorry?'

'You were here yesterday, weren't you?'

'We came to offer our apologies,' said Slater.

'Oh no, you did much more than that,' snapped Randall. 'She called me yesterday and told me you'd been here. She suffers from depression, you know, that's why she gave up her job. You came here asking questions and you've tipped her over the edge. She tried to kill herself once before, you know.'

'Mr Randall, there's nothing anywhere in your wife's service record to suggest she ever suffered from depression, or had ever been assessed for any other health issues until suddenly it was given as the reason she resigned. I can believe she suffers from depression as a result of losing her job, but I don't believe it's the real reason she quit.'

'Of course it is,' argued Randall. 'She told me so herself.'

'Well, I'm sorry, Mr Randall, but from what we've been told, your wife was advised to resign before a scandal ruined her career.'

'Scandal? That's rubbish. Who's been spreading these rumours?'

'Why don't we go inside and ask your wife?' suggested Watson.

'She's not here,' said Randall, desperately. 'That's what I'm trying to tell you. She was gone when I got home yesterday evening, and she's been out all night. I've been calling her mobile phone but it just goes straight to voicemail. I have no idea where she is. This is all your fault. You've pushed her too far.'

'Can we come inside and talk about this?' asked Slater. 'I can see you're worried about your wife. Perhaps we can help you find her.'

Reluctantly, Alan Randall stepped back to let them in. 'Now what's this rumour you're spreading, and what reason can you possibly have for poking your nose into my wife's affairs anyway?'

'Perhaps you'd like me to write a list,' said Slater, coldly.

'I can't believe you, Inspector Slater. Don't you know who my wife is? She used to be a detective inspector, just like you!'

'And that means what, exactly?' asked Slater. 'Are you suggesting that because your wife was a DI fourteen years ago, I should turn a blind eye to her suspicious behaviour? That may be how your wife used to work, but I'm afraid that's not how I work.'

'You're just hounding her for the sake of it!'

'No, Mr Randall, we're not hounding her, we're doing our job.'

'But you've got no reason to be doing any of this. She's already told you the body you found isn't our son, and you told her yesterday you have DNA evidence that proves who the parents are.'

'It's true the DNA evidence proves who the parents are,' agreed Slater, 'but it's not as simple as that.'

'And what's that supposed to mean?'

'When we came here the first time, we showed you both some photographs,' said Watson. 'One of those photos was

152

of a pendant found around the dead child's neck. We believe your wife recognised that pendant.'

'Rubbish!' snapped Randall.

'We believe the pendant is a family piece that was originally given to Diana's great-grandmother and has been passed down through the generations. Diana is Catholic, isn't she?' asked Watson.

'What about you, Mr Randall, did you recognise the pendant?' asked Slater.

'My wife already told you, there must be thousands of those pendants.'

'According to the makers, they actually made around five hundred,' said Slater.

'Well, that's plenty, isn't it? Perhaps it was taken from our son and given to this dead boy.'

'Ah, so now you're saying it *is* Diana's pendant?' asked Slater.

'I'm saying no such thing,' said Randall. 'Don't you dare try to put words into my mouth, Inspector!'

Watson looked across at Slater and he nodded. 'When exactly was your son born, Mr Randall?' she asked. 'Only we don't seem to be able to find any record of your wife ever having taken any maternity leave.'

'She didn't take any maternity leave because she was in line for promotion. I worked from home so it was quite practical for me to look after the baby.'

'So you put your career on hold so she could keep on climbing the greasy pole,' said Slater. 'That was very good of you.'

'I was happy to do it,' said Randall. 'You do these things for people you love.'

'I bet you must have been overjoyed when she decided to quit less than five years later.'

'I told you, she was suffering from depression. It wasn't a question of choice.'

'And I've told you there's no mention of depression anywhere in her records until she resigned.'

Slater was staring at Randall, but the other man couldn't maintain eye contact and soon looked away.

'When was this, Mr Randall?' asked Watson.

Randall had to think hard before he spoke. 'In 2000.'

'And what, she just popped the baby out one day and then went back to work?'

'Don't be absurd. Of course she had a few days off to recover.'

Watson shook her head. 'Sorry, Mr Randall, but like I said a couple of minutes ago, there's no record of your wife ever having taken any maternity leave.'

'There must be some mistake.'

'There's no mistake,' said Watson, with a sad little smile. 'You see, there's also no record of your wife ever having had a baby. No baby, no maternity leave.'

A look of horror took control of Randall's face for a few seconds, and then he shook his head. 'My God, you *have* got it in for her, haven't you?' he asked sadly, his voice almost a whisper. 'Why are you doing this?

'You didn't answer the question, Mr Randall,' said Slater.

Randall gave Slater a look of sheer loathing. 'If anything happens to her it'll be on your head.'

'Yes, I'm sure it will,' said Slater.

'I thought you said you were going to help find her, but you're not interested in that at all, are you?'

'Actually, Mr Randall, I really do want to find Diana, and I promise you we'll be doing our very best to find her, but first you need to give us some answers. Why is it we can find no record of your wife ever having had a baby?'

'Because the poor woman can't have children!' snapped Randall, glaring at Slater. 'There, now you know. We adopted our son, all right?'

'Ah! I see,' said Slater. 'So why have we only just been told this? Why not tell us that from the start instead of giving us a load of bull about her having a baby? And why is there no mention of this in the original inquiry into your son's disappearance?'

'Because it makes no bloody difference, does it? The poor kid was snatched. Who the birth parents are makes no difference whatsoever.'

'So now I understand why you didn't want to give us DNA samples,' said Slater.

Randall said nothing.

'Tell him, Watson,' said Slater.

Randall looked surprised. 'Tell me what?'

'There's no record of you ever adopting a child,' said Watson, 'but you knew that already, didn't you?'

'I don't think I'm going to answer any more questions without my lawyer.' said Randall.

'I think that's probably a good idea,' said Slater. 'In the meantime, I've arranged for you to be taken to Flipton Police Station where you will be held for further questioning. You can contact your solicitor from there.'

'What about my wife? Are you going to find her?'

'Don't worry, Mr Randall,' said Slater. 'I can promise you we're going to be looking everywhere for her.'

CHAPTER THIRTY-FOUR

'D'you think he's going to tell us much more?' asked Watson as they began yet another three-hour drive back to their hotel at Ramlinstoke.

'Unless I'm very much mistaken, that's about all we're going to get right now,' said Slater. 'I think he's realised that without Diana there to tell him what to do, he's already told us a lot more than he should have.'

'That was good of DCI Lipton to help us out like that.'

'Don't forget it was his case originally, and he didn't solve it,' said Slater. 'I think that's why he wants to help. He always thought the Randalls weren't very helpful, but he didn't realise how much they were keeping back.'

'But if his mob had done their job properly in the first place, they could have discovered the same information as us,' said Watson.

'Well, yeah,' admitted Slater, reluctantly, 'but then Diana was one of their own, why wouldn't they take her at face value? Unlike us, they also didn't know anything about Kylie Mason and David Hudson.'

'Even so, it should all have been checked as a matter of course,' insisted Watson.

'Lipton knows that,' said Slater.

'Is he trying to buy you off by being helpful now?' asked Watson.

'I don't think so. He knows we won't hide anything when we come to write our report.'

Watson gave him a pointed look, and he couldn't help but grin. 'Okay, I stand corrected, he knows we won't hide anything when *you* come to write our report, which I will then read through before signing.'

Slater watched from the corner of his eye as Watson's frown morphed into a smile. He didn't mind that she wanted to make sure they both acknowledged how things were really going to work around here, and anyway, he hated writing reports.

'I think Lipton genuinely wants to help because he thinks he should, not because he's hoping to gain some sort of advantage by it.'

Watson seemed happy to accept Slater's opinion of Lipton and his motive. 'So d'you really think Sonny Randall was actually Kylie Mason's son?' she asked.

'It's a possibility that has crossed my mind,' admitted Slater. 'He had to have been somewhere for all those years, and the Randalls don't seem to be able to explain how they come to have a son.'

'Yes, but how?' asked Watson.

'Maybe they bought him,' said Slater.

'You mean an unofficial adoption? But that sort of thing tends to involve orphans from abroad.'

'I was thinking even more unofficial than that.'

'You mean kids stolen to order?' asked a horrified Watson.

'Why not?'

'You'd have to pay a premium price for a service like that.'

'Money doesn't appear to be a problem, does it?'

'Yes, but even so, stolen babies? That's going beyond the pale, isn't it?'

Slater shrugged his shoulders. 'Okay, so not necessarily stolen to order, but what about this for a scenario? Suppose you're the sort of person who will stoop to any level. You know someone who's desperate for a kid, has money, and has approached you because she knows you can supply what she wants. Then one day you get an opportunity to take a baby. What do you do?'

Watson thought about this scenario for a couple of minutes. 'But we know Kylie was run down by a car.'

'Thereby creating just the opportunity I'm talking about,' said Slater.

'You mean I run her down on purpose? Murder as well as kidnapping?'

'Why not, if the money's right?'

'But if I was the driver, how would I make sure I didn't kill the baby too?'

'Maybe the baby's in a pushchair and you can knock down Kylie without touching the pushchair.'

'David Hudson said Kylie used to carry the baby in a sling.'

'Okay,' said Slater. 'So you knock down Kylie, maybe even by accident, yet somehow the baby survives.'

'Now you're relying on good fortune and not murder,' said Watson.

'You just sounded as if you weren't keen on murder.'

'I'm not, but couldn't I just take a baby from somewhere?'

'Of course,' agreed Slater. 'But you want minimal risk. Kylie was out late at night on a quiet country road.'

'What, and I knew she was going to be there?'

'Okay, so it was an opportunist crime.'

'This is getting too far-fetched,' said Watson.

'Maybe,' said Slater, 'but don't forget, you're going out of your way to think up reasons why it can't work. There are just as many reasons why it does work.'

Watson considered this for another minute or so. 'All right,' she conceded, eventually. 'It's a crazy idea, but it might explain how Sonny came to end up with the Randalls. But how does he come to end up over a hundred miles from home in a ditch alongside his real mother?'

Slater glanced at Watson and smiled.

'Don't tell me you've worked that one out, too,' said Watson.

'It's just an idea,' said Slater. 'What if Diana Randall had found out where she could buy a kid because she was a DI?'

'You mean she turned a blind eye rather than paid money?'

Slater looked across at Watson again. 'You're getting the hang of this "what if" game, aren't you?' he said, appreciatively. 'I hadn't actually considered that, but it's certainly a possibility.'

'What was your idea, then?'

'What I was thinking was maybe the person she got the kid from knew she was a DI and decided to blackmail her. It works with your blind eye scenario too.'

'So, she was being blackmailed,' said Watson, taking up where Slater had stopped, 'but what, she stopped paying and the blackmailer took Sonny?'

'That would work,' said Slater, 'because if the blackmailer was the person who ran Kylie down and shoved her into that ditch, he would have known where to bury Sonny so that if he was ever found, the other one would be, too.'

'But what would I gain by that?'

'I dunno,' conceded Slater. 'If my theory's going to work we've still got to work that bit out.' He thought for a few seconds more before adding, 'Or maybe I'm just over-thinking this whole thing.'

'But something like that just might explain why Diana quit her job,' suggested Watson. 'Maybe the thought of the blackmailer exposing her secret was the real reason, and the rumoured affair was just a diversion.'

They drove on in silence for the next five minutes, both considering the merits of the theory they had developed.

'Of course, it's all pure conjecture,' said Slater, at last. 'I doubt we could prove any of it right now.'

'I have a question,' said Watson. 'Where does the anonymous tip-off come into it?'

'Maybe it was the blackmailer, because Diana had stopped paying,' Slater said.

'But I thought that's why Sonny was taken.'

'Uh? Oh yeah,' conceded Slater, gloomily. 'I thought that was all coming together rather too easily. But then, like I said, it might all be pie in the sky anyway if we can't prove Sonny really was Kylie's son.'

'Is this how you solve all your cases?' asked Watson.

Slater chuckled, quietly. 'What, brainstorming? Once in a while I get it right, but to be honest Norm's much better at it than me. He's as sharp as a knife, whereas I rely on lucky guesses.'

'Oh, I'm not letting the side down, am I?' asked Watson, sounding disappointed.

'Don't be bloody daft, Sam,' said Slater. 'How could you possibly match Norm's thirty years' experience when you're not much more than thirty years old?'

'But it must be very different for you with him not being here.'

'Oh, it is, believe me,' said Slater. 'If Norm was here now, my car would be like a rubbish tip. Our office would look as if a bomb had hit it and it would take me hours to find anything.'

'But I thought you got on so well.'

'We do,' said Slater, 'but he still used to drive me to distraction with his untidiness. And, I suspect if I'm working with you and it comes to a chase, there would be two of us running after the fugitive, right?'

'Well, yes, of course.'

'So that's another thing, Norm didn't do running.'

'Ah,' said Watson, 'so if you chased someone down and got into a sticky situation—'

'I'd be on my own,' finished Slater.

'That's not so good,' admitted Watson.

'Norm's name should be on Bradshaw's list,' said Slater, fondly. 'His brain works fine, but the rest of him? Well . . .'

'I see,' said Watson.

'I don't ever want to hear you comparing yourself to anyone I've worked with before,' said Slater. 'It's a pointless exercise because we can't turn the clock back, and even if I could, I wouldn't want to. I took this job knowing I was going to be working with you, and I'll have you know I'm very happy with the way things are working out.'

'Oh, right, I see.' A faint blush was creeping across Watson's face once again.

'And when it comes to brainstorming,' said Slater, 'experience isn't always a blessing. Sometimes it gets in the way.'

'But without evidence, it's all guesswork anyway, isn't it?'

Slater laughed. 'Ha! Sometimes it's guesswork even *with* evidence. But you're right, guesswork and a bit of luck comes into it far more than anyone cares to admit.'

Watson fished in her bag and produced her notebook and pen. 'Right,' she said, opening the book, 'so what do we need the team to look out for next? Maybe we can get lucky through them.'

'Let's start with the Randalls' bank statements for 2000 and 2001,' suggested Slater.

'How about any cases Diana worked on at Flipton that might have involved someone who is suspected of trafficking people?'

'Yep, that's a good one,' agreed Slater, 'and get them to find Diana's medical records. Let's see if Alan was telling the truth about her not being able to have kids.'

'Anything else?' asked Watson, picking up her mobile phone.

'Yes, ask them to chase up Colin Norton's phone records!'

A couple of minutes later, Watson ended her call and turned to Slater.

'A copy of Colin Norton's phone records will be in your inbox when you get back,' she said. 'Apparently there's one number he calls rather a lot. They've traced it back to a mobile owned by Diana Randall.'

'Excellent,' said Slater. 'Now we're beginning to get somewhere.'

'And they're going to see if they can track her by her mobile phone.'

CHAPTER THIRTY-FIVE

It was obvious from Colin Norton's phone records that he had called Diana Randall less than fifteen minutes after Slater and Watson had last spoken to him, and three more times since. 'I would suggest that's how she knew we would be coming back,' said Slater.

'But he can't know how much we know,' said Watson, 'so I wonder what he's told her?'

'All he knew was that we were investigating the body found in the ditch and we'd linked it to David Hudson,' said Slater. 'But Hudson came to town after Diana had left, so why would he need to tell her anything about it?'

He studied the list of calls. 'Now this is interesting. He called Diana on 22 October.'

'That's the day the police got the tip-off. Do you think he called to tell her about that?'

'It's a bit of a coincidence, isn't it?'

'D'you think we need to pay him another visit?'

'I think so, don't you?' said Slater. 'We could go back to the hotel via his house. You weren't doing anything tonight were you?'

Watson pretended to consider her options for a minute before replying. 'Well, I was going to wash my hair, but that will have to wait, I can't turn down an offer like that!'

* * *

Colin Norton lived in a dingy basement flat. He wasn't best pleased when he opened his front door to find Slater and Watson on his doorstep. 'Oh, God, what do you want now?'

Slater gave him a humourless smile. 'Good evening, Colin, nice to see you too. I'm so pleased we caught you at home.'

'Yeah, I bet you are,' said Norton. 'But I'm going out soon, so you can clear off.'

'This will only take five minutes,' said Slater.

'Well, go on, then, ask away,' said Norton.

'Aw, come on, Colin, it's starting to rain out here.'

'Well, that's your bad luck. Don't say I didn't offer you the chance to ask your questions.' He started to close the door, but Slater stepped forward and planted a foot firmly in place to stop it. 'Now, now, Colin, you can let us in and we can make this a pleasant chat, or we can go down to your nick, in front of your mates, and take all night. Take your pick.' He finished with his crocodile smile.

Norton looked like he was mulling it over. It occurred to Slater that Norton was unlikely to have any mates down at the station.

'You've got five minutes and that's it!' he said eventually, opening the door.

'That will be plenty of time, Colin,' said Slater. 'We've only got a couple of questions.'

They followed him down a dark hallway and into a living room with decor that had obviously been inspired by the dampness and decay that was a feature of Norton's home. The musty odour of mildew seemed to be everywhere.

'Oh, this is nice,' said Slater, with heavy sarcasm.

'Take a seat,' said Norton, ignoring Slater's jibe.

Slater looked at the seats on offer then looked at Watson. Her expression told him exactly what she thought of that idea.

'I think we prefer to stand,' said Slater. 'Mildew's a bugger to get off your clothes.'

'I don't choose to live in this shithole,' said Norton. 'When your ex-wife is taking almost every penny you bring home in the name of child support, you have to live where you can.'

'You're divorced?' asked Slater, trying to sound surprised. 'That's a shame, can I ask why?'

'It was just one of those things,' said Norton. 'People grow apart sometimes.'

'It was adultery, wasn't it?' asked Slater.

Norton looked daggers at him.

Slater shrugged his shoulders in apology. 'Lucky guess,' he said, 'I heard a rumour, you see, about you and a DS you used to work with years ago.'

'You don't wanna believe everything you hear,' said Norton. 'People often put two and two together and end up with the wrong answer.'

'That's true enough, but sometimes they get the answer spot on,' said Slater. 'We have a witness who claims you and Diana Randall made a habit of going missing if you were on duty together.'

'That's cobblers,' snapped Norton. 'Anyway, that was twenty years ago. Even now you can still hit patches where there's no signal.'

'D'you still keep in touch?'

'Now and then,' conceded Norton.

'Would you say you were good friends?' asked Slater.

'Not really.'

'Yet when her son went missing, you were there the very next day volunteering to join the searches. That suggests you were a very good friend.'

'We worked together. Anyone normal would have done the same,' explained Norton.

'Anyone normal who wasn't a good friend would probably have lost touch after six years,' said Slater, 'yet Diana called you and told you her son was missing.'

Norton licked his lips, eyes darting between Slater and Watson. 'I saw it on the daily bulletin, missing persons.'

'Oh, right, of course, I didn't think of that,' said Slater. 'So what happened then, did you ask for leave there and then?'

'Yeah, that's right,' said Norton, seeming relieved that Slater had given him a way out.

Slater nodded to Watson who opened her bag and withdrew a sheaf of paper.

'What's this?' asked Norton.

'Your mobile phone records,' said Slater, watching the colour drain from Norton's face as he realised he'd been caught out. 'What? Did you think we'd be too stupid to check your phone? It seems you make more than an occasional phone call to Diana Randall. I would say you call her a lot, wouldn't you?'

'So? We're friends and we keep in touch. There's no law against that, is there?'

'Not at all,' said Slater. 'Can you tell me why you called her on 22 October?'

'I can't remember. Probably just for a chat, see how she was, that sort of thing.'

'So, there was no specific reason?'

'I don't think so,' said Norton, carefully.

Slater gave Norton a cold, hard stare, but it only seemed to succeed in making him more stubborn.

'We haven't got the records all the way back to the time Sonny Randall went missing yet,' said Slater, 'but I think we're going to find a lot of calls between you and Diana around that time, don't you? That seems to be a bit odd, considering you weren't really good friends, don't you think?'

'I don't know what you're getting at,' said Norton. 'Diana and Alan had lost their son and I tried to help find him. What's wrong with that?'

'Oh, so it's Diana and Alan? You're friends with both of them? Does Alan know you were having an affair with his wife?'

'We were *not* having an affair,' snapped Norton.

'My witness seems pretty convinced you were.'

'Well, your witness is mistaken.'

'Do you recall when her son was born?' asked Slater. 'As a family friend, I expect you knew all about it.'

Norton had looked uncomfortable from the minute they had arrived, but now he looked distinctly concerned. 'No, I didn't know all about it,' he mumbled. 'I didn't find out until some time after.'

'But I thought you were a family friend?'

'When they moved up to Flipton I lost touch for a while. It was two or three years before we got back in touch.'

'I expect she missed your dazzling wit and repartee,' said Slater, but the comment went straight over Norton's head unnoticed.

'Were you surprised when you found out she had a baby?' asked Watson.

'I was surprised when she gave up her job to look after the boy. That was supposed to be Alan's job, he was the one who wanted a kid so badly.'

'So Diana didn't want a baby?' asked Watson. 'Why not?'

'Because she was a career girl, heading for the top! Now, you've had your five minutes and I'm supposed to be somewhere, so if you wouldn't mind?'

'Fair enough,' said Slater. 'But don't leave town, we're going to want to speak to you again.'

'I'll look forward to it,' said Norton.

CHAPTER THIRTY-SIX

When Slater woke next morning, he still hadn't heard from Jenny, but he had decided if she wanted to play games, that was up to her. Whatever she was up to, she wasn't going to distract him from doing his job.

Something important was nagging away at him, but he couldn't put his finger on what exactly it was. By the time they got to the office, it had become an itch he just had to scratch, but the problem was, he had no idea where to start. In the end, he decided to begin at the beginning. Sonny Randall's disappearance was the first file they had collected, so he started there.

He skimmed through the reports once again, and then turned his attention to the various photographs. He got to his feet and spread them out on the longest worktop. Then he stepped back and took a long look at each one in turn, finally coming back to the photograph of Sonny's bike. His intuition had told him this photograph was important, and he tried to focus everything he had upon it, but for the life of him, he couldn't see what he was looking for.

'Sir?' called Watson.

'Mmm?'

'I think you need to see this. The team have got hold of Diana's medical records.'

'They haven't managed to find her, have they?' he asked as he turned to join her.

'Sorry,' she said. 'It seems her mobile phone is switched off.'

'Yeah, she'd know we could track her with it,' said Slater. 'How about using the ANPR system to try and track the car?'

'They're moving on to that next,' said Watson. 'I've got her photo everywhere but so far no sightings.'

Slater was looking over her shoulder now. 'So what have they found in the medical records? Was Alan telling the truth about her not being able to have kids?'

'Not according to this,' she said. 'There's nothing to say she couldn't have children. In fact, there's evidence to prove the exact opposite. She had an abortion in March 2000!'

'What? Are they sure that's right?'

'Colin Norton said she was a career girl.'

'But Alan Randall said she wanted kids but was unable to have any. Now why would he tell us she couldn't have kids if she could?'

'Maybe she told him that, and he believed her. She did seem to be the boss.'

'But why would you have an abortion if you wanted kids?'

'She was a career girl,' repeated Watson. 'Maybe she felt the time wasn't right to put her career on hold. Don't forget, she won her promotion at the end of that year. You said yourself, she wouldn't have got it if she was pregnant.'

'There's another possibility,' said Slater. 'Alan Randall's older than Diana, right? But he's also loaded. What if she married him for his money but didn't much fancy having sex with him? Don't forget she's got Colin the sex machine for that. So she tells Alan she can't have kids, and maybe even uses that as some sort of excuse for not having sex with him. But then she unexpectedly finds she's pregnant. Alan's going to know it's not his, and anyway, she's told him she can't have kids, so she takes a few days off, visits one of those clinics, and Bob's your uncle. And Alan never knows anything about it.'

'Are you going to ask him?' asked Watson.

'Who? Norton or Randall?'

'Well, both I suppose,' said Watson. 'But it's going to be a bit difficult with Randall being three hours away.'

'That's the trouble with being mobile,' said Slater. 'We don't really have the facilities for holding anyone, do we? DCI Lipton has offered to interview Randall for us, but I'd much rather we do it ourselves, if we can.'

'What about Norton?' asked Watson. 'Are we going to question him about this?'

'Yes we are, and I want to know more about why he called her on 22 October. Was it really a coincidence, or was there some reason she needed to know about the tip-off?'

'So who's going to be first?' asked Watson.

Slater thought for a moment. 'Let me call Lipton and see what he says, and then we'll decide.' He turned towards his own desk. 'Tell the team well done, won't you?'

As he turned away from Watson, his eyes were drawn back to the photograph he had been studying before. Now he could see what had been bothering him. 'Have you got a minute, Sam? Come and have a look at this photograph and tell me what you see.'

Watson spun her chair round and took the two steps across to where Slater had laid out the photos. He pointed to the photo. 'This one here.'

Watson looked at the photo. 'I see a kid's bike.'

'What else? Give me a bit more detail.'

She turned a confused look in his direction.

'It's all right, you're doing fine,' he said, to reassure her. 'I didn't see it at first. In fact, I've been staring at it for ages without spotting it, and then you called me, and when I came back I spotted it straight away.'

She looked back at the photo again. 'But it's just a little bike, parked up on its stand, at the side of the lane.'

'Exactly!' said Slater. 'It's neatly parked at the side of the lane. So who left it like that?'

'Well, Sonny, I suppose,' said Watson.

'But we've been told he was snatched. When kids are snatched, it's a rushed job. There's not time for either the kid or the kidnapper to worry about the bike, especially the kid, who's terrified. The bike doesn't get neatly parked, it gets tossed to one side, doesn't it?'

'Yes, I see what you mean,' said Watson. 'If Sonny had time to park the bike at the side of the lane, up on its stand, that suggests he was in no great hurry.'

'Right,' said Slater. 'I think he knew whoever took him, and went willingly with them. This wasn't a random snatch — it was either planned by someone who knew the family—'

'Or by one, or both, parents,' finished Watson.

'Right,' said Slater, 'so that's another question for Alan Randall and Diana, when we find her. Let's get up straight here, then go and see Norton. Maybe someone will have spotted Diana by then.'

As Watson reached her desk, her laptop pinged to signal the arrival of yet another email. 'This is interesting,' she said, reading the message. 'I thought it was highly unlikely Norton would have been able to book time off at short notice, like he claimed for when Sonny disappeared, so I did some checking. It appears our Colin is a creature of habit. He books the same weeks off every year and has done for as long as anyone can remember. He didn't have to ask for time off when Sonny disappeared, he was already on leave.'

'Christ,' said Slater. 'If he was on leave, he wouldn't have seen the daily bulletin.'

'So either Diana told him Sonny had been abducted, or he already knew!' said Watson. 'I wonder if Sonny knew him well enough to trust him? But why would he take him?'

'Right, decision made,' said Slater. 'Let's go and see Norton first. I can call Lipton on the way.'

CHAPTER THIRTY-SEVEN

'It appears Bradshaw has been pulling strings in the background. Lipton is sending Alan Randall down here,' said Slater as he finished his call and slipped his mobile phone into his pocket.

'That'll make life easier,' said Watson, as she eased the car into a vacant space close to Ramlinstoke Police Station.

'But it's not making us very popular with Randall's solicitor,' said Slater. 'Apparently he's filing a complaint about the way we're treating his client, and he intends to get his client released forthwith.'

'Ah,' said Watson, 'that's not so good.'

'Yeah, well, Bradshaw doesn't seem to be unduly concerned. He suggested we just carry on regardless, and he'll deal with the shit when it actually hits the fan. Does that sound about right?'

'Yes, he's not fazed by much,' said Watson. 'This wouldn't be the first time we've ruffled a few feathers.'

'Shake the tree and let's see what falls out,' said Slater with a wry smile. 'It works for me!'

They climbed from the car and made the short walk into the reception area at Ramlinstoke Police Station. A desk sergeant was perched on a stool behind the counter, studiously ignoring them. Watson marched over and flashed her warrant card. He managed a cursory glance. 'I'm DS Brearley,' she announced. 'We'd like to have a few words with DS Colin Norton.'

The sergeant was unimpressed. 'And why would you want to talk to him?'

'He's been helping us with an inquiry,' explained Watson.

'Oh, so you're the mob over at Trillington, are you? I'm not sure I should be helping you lot.'

'And why's that?'

'Apparently we're not good enough to investigate a case right here on our own doorstep, so I doubt—'

'What's your name, Sergeant?' snapped Slater.

'Smith.'

'Well, listen up, Sergeant Smith, just like you, we don't get to choose what comes through that front door, we don't get to pick and choose what cases we get, and just like you, we have to get on with whatever gets thrown at us. I'm sorry if the fact we've been given a case on your doorstep offends you, but that's how it is, so I suggest you deal with it. You're supposed to be a professional, so why don't you grow up and try to act like one.'

Smith drew himself up from his seat and looked down his nose at Slater. He stood about six feet four, so he towered over him. 'And who the hell are you to be telling me what to do?' he boomed.

Slater slapped his own warrant card down on the counter. 'Slater, detective inspector,' he said, quietly.

Smith looked down at the warrant card and then back up to Slater. He swallowed noisily. 'Oh, right, well, I suppose that's different then.'

'I suppose that's different then, sir,' corrected Slater. 'Whatever you might think about us, Sergeant, you will show respect to my rank and to my colleague, who is a fellow police officer trying to do her job, okay?'

'Yes, sir, of course.'

'So where is DS Norton?' asked Watson.

'You'll be wasting your time,' warned Smith.

'Yes, well, that's going to be our problem, not yours,' said Watson.

'You'll find him at the county hospital,' said Smith, 'in the Intensive Care Unit.'

'What's he doing there?' asked Watson in surprise.

'Trying to stay alive, I reckon. The poor bugger got run down last night by a hit-and-run driver. He's in a coma right now.'

'Oh, shit,' hissed Slater.

'Yeah, "oh shit" is right,' agreed Smith, with a sad smile. 'He's not exactly Mr Popularity around here, but even so, no one would wish that on him.'

'No, of course not,' said Slater. 'Any witnesses?'

'Just one of our young detectives, DC Pinkley. He was meeting Norton for a drink and a game of darts. But he was a fair distance away when it happened, and the light wasn't much good.'

'Have you got a description of the car or driver?' asked Slater.

'We've got part of the registration number, and I can tell you it was a dark-coloured saloon, but that's about it. We've got everyone out looking for it, but so far there's no sign.'

'Give us what you've got,' said Slater. 'Another two pairs of eyes can't hurt, unless you've got a problem with that.'

'No, I don't have a problem with that,' said Smith as he passed Slater a photocopied sheet of paper. 'That's everything we've got so far.'

'Right, well, we'll keep our eyes open,' said Slater.

'Thank you, sir. Can I just apologise for earlier—'

'I'm not going to make a big deal out of it, Sergeant,' said Slater. 'Let's put it down to stress. When something like this happens to a colleague, it's bound to upset everyone.'

'Right, thank you, sir.'

* * *

There were police officers everywhere when Slater and Watson got to the hospital. Slater was in two minds about whether they should leave quietly or risk more hostility by going inside. In the end, he decided it wouldn't hurt to see if they could find out how Norton was and when they might be able to speak to him.

'Maybe it's best if I go up there on my own,' he said once they had got their bearings. 'Two strangers are probably going to attract more attention.'

'Okay,' said Watson. 'I'll have a wander around down here and see if I can learn anything.'

Slater made his way quietly up the two floors to the ICU. There was a uniformed officer outside one of the rooms and another three men in suits huddled in a corner drinking coffee, talking in hushed voices. Slater guessed they must be CID officers. He quietly slipped past them and made his way to the nurses' station, further along the corridor.

He flashed his warrant card and asked if he could have a quick update on Colin Norton's condition, but before the nurse could start to tell him, a voice cut in from behind him. 'That's all right, nurse, I'm sure you've got plenty to do. I can bring him up to speed.'

Slater turned to find a man about his own size standing there, arms folded. 'I'm Detective Inspector Styles,' said the man. 'That looked like a warrant card you showed the nurse, but I don't recognise you from around here. Can I ask who you are and what you're doing?'

'DI Slater.' He produced his warrant card again. He looked along the corridor and noticed the other two detectives had gone.

DI Styles took Slater's card and studied it. 'And what's your interest in DS Norton?'

Slater could understand where Styles was coming from. He would have been exactly the same. 'It's a long story,' he said.

'That's all right,' said Styles, with a false smile. 'I've got plenty of time.'

'I'm leading the investigation out at Trillington,' said Slater.

'The body in the ditch?'

'I suppose you're going to give me a hard time about me working a case on your patch now, are you?'

'Believe it or not, Slater,' said Styles, with a broad grin, 'I'm probably the only one at Ramlinstoke who isn't pissed off about you being there. The moaning minnies seem to forget we haven't got enough people to cope with our current caseload without getting lumbered with something from twenty years ago. But what does that have to do with Colin Norton?'

'Is there somewhere we can get a cup of coffee?' asked Slater.

'Good idea,' said Styles. 'There's a cafeteria one floor down. Follow me.'

* * *

It was good half hour before Slater got back to his car and the waiting Watson. 'Sorry about that,' he said as he climbed into the car. 'I got caught by the guy leading the investigation, DI Styles. He wanted to know why we wanted to speak to Norton, and why we've put out an alert for Diana Randall, so I had to let him into a bit of our case, but at least I got some information back in return. It turns out Colin Norton has sustained—'

'Severe internal injuries and multiple fractures, including a fractured skull,' finished Watson. 'And now he's in a coma.'

'How did you find that out?' asked Slater.

'The guy he was meeting for a drink, DC Stewart Pinkley. He's in bits. I found him outside having a cigarette. The poor guy's only a youngster, and he's never seen a battered body before last night. He told me he was a good forty or fifty yards away when he saw Norton walking towards him. As Norton started to cross the road, this car suddenly accelerated down the road from behind him and just drove straight through him as if he wasn't there.'

'Did he think it was deliberate or an accident?'

'Deliberate. He says he's quite sure the car had been there for a few minutes, and the driver didn't start the engine until Norton had passed it.'

'So, whoever was driving was waiting for him?'

'That's what Pinkley reckons.'

'Male or female driver?'

'Too dark to see.'

'What about the colour of the car?' asked Slater. 'Is he sure it was blue?'

'I made sure to ask him that,' said Watson. 'He says it could have been black, or even dark green, but he was more focused on trying to help Norton than studying the car.'

'Styles wanted to know if we thought Diana Randall had run down Colin Norton.'

'What did you tell him?'

'There was no point in denying it's a possibility,' said Slater, gloomily. 'Styles is no fool. He would have worked it out for himself soon enough.'

'So now we're all looking for the same fugitive,' said Watson. 'I suppose at least that improves the chances of finding her.'

'Yeah, but it also means they're going to get first dibs at questioning her when she's found. And as their case is current, and it's their police station, I suspect we'll have a long wait, so we'd best make sure we find out what we can from Alan Randall when he gets here.'

'When's that?' asked Watson.

'I'm told around three this afternoon, so while we're waiting, why don't we go and see Ted Rivers again? Maybe he can recall something that might help us.'

CHAPTER THIRTY-EIGHT

'They both denied they were having an affair, of course,' Slater told Ted Rivers. 'Norton claimed there are still blind spots where you can lose radio contact even today.'

'Well, you didn't think they were going to admit it, did you?' asked Rivers.

'I was wondering if there was anything else you can remember that might help us,' said Slater.

'Such as?'

'Anything you can tell us about the last few weeks she was at Ramlinstoke? What frame of mind she was in?'

'I'll tell you one thing,' said Rivers. 'She didn't seem all that happy for someone who had landed a job like that at such a young age.'

'You mean she was having second thoughts?' asked Slater.

'Or maybe she just couldn't wait to start her new job and didn't want to be there any more,' suggested Watson.

'I don't think it was either of those,' said Rivers. 'She seemed sort of distracted, like she had some big decision on her mind.'

'Getting cold feet at the last minute isn't that unusual,' said Slater. 'She was still young, and it was big change coming her way.'

'Oh, this wasn't just at the last minute,' said Rivers. 'She was like it all summer up until the time she left.'

Watson gave Slater a look that suggested she had just solved the last clue of *The Times* crossword, but if so, he thought she was way ahead of him. 'What about the week she left?' he asked. 'I take it there was a bit of a party?'

'Yes, that's right,' recalled Rivers. 'She came back for her party. I remember now, she had some leave in between jobs and she arranged her leaving party so she wouldn't have to worry about getting up for work next day.'

'When would that have been?' asked Slater.

Rivers looked at Slater with an amused glint in his eye. 'You don't seriously expect me to remember exact dates, do you? It was years ago! I know she finished on a Friday, and the party was the following Friday.'

'And she drove all the way back home after a party?' asked Slater. 'I didn't have her down as a non-drinker.'

'Oh, she can drink all right,' said Rivers. 'Whether she drove home that night, I don't know. Perhaps she booked a hotel room so she wouldn't have to drive home. Now I'm talking about it, I'm sure I remember her and Norton did the disappearing thing that night too, only this time they never reappeared. If she was booked into a hotel somewhere, maybe she took him back there.'

* * *

'What was that look you gave me in there?' asked Slater as soon as they were back in the car.

'What look?' asked Watson, innocently.

'The one that said you know something I don't.'

'Oh, that look. Well, she had an abortion in March that year, yes? It might have seemed a good idea at the time, but what if she then had second thoughts? Maybe she found her hormones were telling her that actually she wanted that baby more than she wanted the promotion. She wouldn't be the first woman to regret having an abortion.'

178

Slater smiled his appreciation for Watson's thinking. 'That would explain why Rivers thought she was preoccupied,' he said. 'And if she was feeling really desperate, maybe she approached someone who could provide what she wanted.'

'It certainly fits the theory,' agreed Watson.

'What date did she finish at Ramlinstoke? Was it 15 October?'

'Yes, I think so.'

'So the party would have been on 22 October?'

Watson looked his way and they exchanged a look. 'The same date Kylie was run down.'

'Exactly,' said Slater. 'Come on, let's go and see if Alan Randall's back yet. I think we have some questions for him.'

CHAPTER THIRTY-NINE

The first thing Slater and Watson saw as they pushed their way through the front doors into Ramlinstoke Police Station was Sergeant Smith perched on his usual stool behind the counter. They might have called a truce last time they met, but the smirk on Smith's face told Slater he knew something they weren't going to be happy about.

'Afternoon, Sergeant Smith,' said Slater. 'We're expecting a prisoner to be delivered here for questioning this afternoon. Can you tell us if he's arrived yet?'

'Afternoon, sir,' said Smith as he picked up a clipboard from his desk and made a big deal of looking through the notes on it. 'Oh yes, Alan Randall, is that him?'

'That's the one.'

'He's in interview room two,' said Smith, his grin widening. 'DI Styles is with him at the moment. He left instructions for you to wait here until he's finished, and then he'll come and find you.'

Slater was beside himself. 'But he's our bloody suspect,' he snapped.

'Yes, sir,' agreed Smith, 'but I think Mr Styles feels our hit-and-run case involving one of our own officers, who's still just about alive, takes priority over your old skeletons.'

'Oh for God's sake,' said Slater, in frustration, his face beginning to redden. Watson could see trouble ahead if she didn't do something.

'As you told me yourself, sir,' continued Smith, 'that's how it is, so I suggest—'

'I wouldn't finish that sentence, Sergeant,' interrupted Watson. 'You might get away with being smug, but I wouldn't push your luck too far. There is a limit and, right now, you're in grave danger of overstepping it.'

Smith turned his grin on Watson, but it faded as he took in the look on her face. The threat was real.

'Tell DI Styles we're in the canteen,' said Watson. 'We'll have a coffee while we wait.'

She took Slater's arm and directed him away from the counter. 'Come on, sir. If we make a fuss they'll only stall us even longer.'

* * *

Half an hour later, Slater was still brooding when the chair next to him was pulled back and DI Styles sat down next to him. He glared at Styles, who raised his hands in a placatory gesture. 'Look, I know you're pissed off,' he said, 'but I've got an officer in Intensive Care. As far as I'm concerned, that's more important than two skeletons you found in a ditch a few miles away. If the roles were reversed, you would have done exactly the same, and I'd be the one who was pissed off. I know it, and you know it.'

Slater sighed. It was frustrating, but he knew Styles was right, and he knew there was no point in arguing about it. What was done was done. 'Yes, I suppose you're right,' he said. 'It's just that we're so close, you know?'

'Well, he's all yours now,' said Styles. 'We've checked his car against Pinkley's description and it fits the bill. He's also admitted she has the car, although he claims he has no idea where she is. So she's my main suspect in the hit-and-run.'

'We think she could be responsible for a lot more than that,' said Slater.

'Any idea why she'd want to run him down?'

'Twenty years ago, they were lovers. We think it's got something to do with that,' said Slater, vaguely.

'Well, if she's still in the area, it'll be a lot easier to find her with our resources than just the two of you,' said Styles. 'So why don't you share what you know?'

'It's what we *suspect* we know rather than what we *actually* know,' said Slater. 'That's why I need to speak to Alan Randall. Rather than me sitting here talking to you, why don't you observe our interview?'

* * *

Alan Randall had looked rough the last time Slater had seen him, but he looked a whole lot rougher now. Unshaven and unkempt, there was an air of desperation about him, but at least now his solicitor had caught up with him.

'I'd like you to know this is an outrage,' said the solicitor. 'My client strongly denies all charges—'

'No one has made any charges yet, have they?' asked Slater.

'Well, no, but—'

'So it's a bit early to be denying anything, isn't it?'

'Mr Randall couldn't have been driving the car that knocked down the police officer.'

'Yes, we know that,' said Slater. 'We've already established his wife had the car last night. I'm not questioning Mr Randall about DS Norton. I want to question him about his wife's involvement in another matter.'

This seemed to silence the solicitor, for the time being. For all his outrage, he obviously wasn't up to speed with the circumstances behind his client's situation.

'Now then, Mr Randall,' said Slater. 'You understand we believe Diana ran down DS Colin Norton last night, and we're confident when we find your car there will be damage to back up our theory.'

'Poppycock,' snapped Randall.

'If you say so,' said Slater.

'I thought you weren't asking about last night?' asked the solicitor.

'The cases overlap,' said Slater. 'If you'll just let me finish, you'll understand.' He turned his attention back to Randall. 'Now, Alan, when we spoke before, you told us your wife couldn't have children.'

'Yes.'

'But that's not true, is it?'

'What do you mean?'

'There's no mention of it in her medical records,' said Watson. 'That would seem to be a pretty fundamental piece of medical information for a woman, wouldn't you agree?'

'Of course it's in her records!' said Randall, in disbelief. 'It must be. She had treatment.'

'When did you first know about your wife's problem?'

'After we got married. She went to her doctor about it. She was so disappointed when she came home and told me.'

'You didn't go with her?' asked Watson.

'Well, no.'

'So you can't be sure she even went to the doctor.'

'Are you mad?' snapped Randall. 'Why on earth would she have lied about something like that!'

Slater consulted his notes. 'Did you know your wife went to an abortion clinic in March 2000?' asked Slater.

'Don't be ridiculous.'

Watson took a sheet of paper from the folder before her and placed it in front of Randall. 'For the tape, I'm showing Mr Randall a copy of Mrs Randall's receipt for payment to the Braeburn Clinic,' she announced.

Randall quickly scanned the paper. 'But this is absurd. There must be some mistake.'

'It would be absurd if she really wanted children,' said Watson.

'But she was desperate for a child, that's why we adopted Sonny,' said Randall, wringing his hands.

183

'Mm, yes, the adoption,' said Slater. 'We'll come back to how you came to have Sonny in a minute. What can you tell me about your wife's relationship with Colin Norton?'

'I told you before, they worked together.'

'Oh, they did much more than that together, Mr Randall,' said Slater. 'In fact, we believe Colin Norton was the father of the baby your wife aborted back in March 2000. It was a four-teen-week foetus, so it can't have been yours because you were on an environmental expedition in the Antarctic from July to December 2000.'

Randall gaped at Slater as though he had just punched him.

'I'm sorry, Mr Randall, but all this happened while you were away. The thing is, we believe Diana soon regretted having the abortion, and she realised she actually wanted a baby more than she wanted that new job, but you'd already bought the house, and she'd already got the promotion. It was a bit like a speeding train she couldn't get off.'

Randall stared at his hands. His mouth sagged open, and for a few seconds he looked as if all the fight had gone out of him, rather like a deflated balloon. 'This is all lies,' he said, sadly.

'Is it?' asked Slater. 'Did you know Colin Norton's wife divorced him on the grounds of adultery?'

'I've only got your word for that. I don't understand why you're trying to ruin my wife's reputation. She has nothing to do with Colin Norton.'

'I'm sorry to tell you this, but Colin Norton is a regular caller to Diana's mobile phone.'

Randall said nothing. Slater let him stew for a minute or two before he spoke again. 'Tell us about when Sonny disappeared,' said Slater.

Randall turned dull eyes upon Slater. 'It was terrible. We never did find out who snatched him.'

'And you're quite sure he was snatched, are you?'

'What do you mean? Are you going to tell me that was all lies, too?'

'I noticed something about the photographs,' said Slater.

Watson slipped the photo of Sonny's bike from the folder and announced for the tape as she placed it in front of Randall.

'You see the bike? It's far too neatly parked for a snatch,' said Slater. 'You see, when kids get snatched, whatever they were playing with tends to get flung aside, yet here's Sonny's bike, all neatly parked, up on its stand. Now that tells us there was nothing rushed about what happened that day, and we think that's because Sonny knew and trusted the person who abducted him.'

'What are you saying?'

'Did Diana resent giving up her career?' asked Slater. 'Did she blame Sonny, even though it was her own fault she had to resign?'

'Diana loved Sonny. She would never have hurt him. She loved him like he was her own.'

'But he wasn't her own, was he?'

Randall retreated within himself again, refusing to make eye contact with Slater or Watson.

'Did Colin Norton know Sonny?'

'Yes, of course he did. Colin used to play football with him whenever he came to our house.'

'So Sonny would have trusted Colin?'

'What's that got to do with anything?' asked Randall.

'Maybe nothing,' said Slater. 'I'm just curious, that's all.'

'You're not suggesting Colin had anything to do with Sonny's disappearance, are you? He was one of the first to volunteer to help with the searches.'

'Yes, I'm aware of that,' said Slater. 'That was very noble of him, don't you think? Especially after Diana had aborted his baby.'

Randall refused to rise to the bait, so Slater tried a different tack. 'Losing Sonny must have been really hard to deal with,' he said.

'You couldn't possibly imagine,' snapped Randall. 'We were devastated!'

'So you know a little of what it was like for Sonny's real father?' asked Slater.

'What?'

'Well, don't you think he was devastated when someone took his son?'

'Of course, but—'

'We believe he lost his wife at the same time. How do you think he would have felt after that? Someone ran down his wife, took his son, and sold him to you?'

'What? No! It wasn't like that. I didn't buy him. He was there when I got home—' Suddenly Randall stopped talking.

'Do go on, Mr Randall,' said Slater. 'What do you mean he was there when you got home?'

'My client isn't going to answer any more questions at this time,' announced the solicitor. 'I think I need to spend some time with him before he says anything more.'

Slater had been expecting the solicitor to intervene a lot sooner than this, so he wasn't at all surprised by this development. He knew they would get no more from Randall now, and five minutes later, he was taken back to his cell.

CHAPTER FORTY

Slater and Watson were drinking coffee in Styles' office while they waited for him to finish his telephone call. 'I'm told Alan Randall's car has been tracked using ANPR,' he said, putting the phone down. 'We've got it all the way down the motorway and further south. It looks like Diana was driving and it was last caught just outside town.'

'That more or less proves it was her that ran down Norton, then,' said Slater.

'But surely she would have known about ANPR enabling us to track the car,' said Styles.

'Yes, but we weren't looking for her when she was on the way down, were we?' said Slater.

'But she's made it easy for us to build a case proving she was here.'

'Maybe she just doesn't care what we can prove,' said Watson. 'She's seen the statistics. She would have known all along that her son was almost certainly dead, and she might even have had a good idea who was responsible. If something's now happened to prove her suspicions, perhaps all she cares about is revenge, and she doesn't give a damn about being caught.'

They silently pondered Watson's suggestion before Styles changed the subject. 'So what do you think Randall meant when he said Sonny was there when he got home?' he asked.

'Yeah, that's been playing on my mind,' said Slater. 'I was sure they were both in on it and they had paid someone to get a baby for them, but now I'm not so sure.'

'So, what if Diana was heading back home after her leaving party and she brought the baby back with her?' suggested Watson.

'Yeah, but where did she get it from?'

'Well, we know she's not averse to running people down,' said Watson.

'But she could have killed the baby,' said Slater. 'Would she risk killing them both?'

'You're assuming she did it on purpose,' said Watson. 'What if it was an accident? We know she'd been at a party. What if she'd had too much to drink and she came up behind Kylie and didn't see her until it was too late? She knocks Kylie down and kills her, but by some miracle the baby escapes unhurt.'

Slater nodded his approval. 'Now, that's a possibility. She can't report it because she's been drinking and she's got too much to lose, so she pushes Kylie's body into the ditch and takes the baby home with her.'

'You'll need a bit more proof than that,' said Styles, 'but it's an interesting theory. Anyway, I thought you were also suggesting Diana Randall later murdered the boy, is that right?'

'It's another possibility we had considered,' agreed Slater. 'But why would she then drive a hundred miles to dump the body in the same ditch as Kylie Mason? Why do that and risk both bodies being found? It makes no sense. If they hadn't been together in that ditch, we would never have connected them in a million years.'

'I think you need to push Alan Randall a lot harder,' said Styles. 'Find out what he meant when he said the baby was there when he got home.'

'I'm not sure he can tell us what we want to know,' said Slater. 'He might be sharing a house with Diana Randall, but they're not sharing much else that I can see.' He thought for a moment, then addressed Styles. 'You know Colin Norton, what can you tell us about him?'

'I've only been here for three years, but in my opinion he's the sort of guy you'd rather not have around. He just about does enough to keep his job, and that's about it. He has zero personality, and yet, I'm told he once used to be very popular with the ladies.'

'Is he vindictive?' asked Slater.

'He's definitely an "eye for an eye" sort of bloke. He thinks we should be dishing out punishment beatings. It's his idea of justice.'

'D'you think he's capable of blackmail? Only we think someone could have been blackmailing Diana Randall because they knew how she'd come by Sonny. He was close to her then, so he could well have known.'

Styles didn't take long to consider this before he answered. 'I wouldn't be at all surprised.'

'So, if he found out Diana had aborted his baby, d'you think he'd want revenge?'

'I wouldn't put it past him,' said Styles, 'but maybe that's what he was blackmailing her about, and he knew nothing about how she got Sonny.'

'Yes, but if he did know about Sonny, and then he found out about her abortion . . .' Slater left the sentence unfinished.

'If you're suggesting he would have murdered her son, I'm not so sure he would go that far.'

'Maybe he hadn't intended to kill him. Perhaps it was just intended to be a warning but it got out of hand?'

'It's a bit of a stretch, if you ask me,' said Styles.

'But it would give Diana a motive to run him down and try to kill him,' Watson pointed out.

'But why now?' asked Styles. 'If she knew he'd taken her son, why wait until now to get even? Why not go after him when it happened?'

'Maybe she only just found out,' said Slater. 'Perhaps the fact we found the body in the ditch was the proof she needed.'

'But didn't this all start with an anonymous tip-off about a body somewhere in Trillington? Have you any idea who sent that?'

'Not a clue,' admitted Slater. 'It did occur to me that it could have been Norton. Maybe he was blackmailing Diana and she stopped paying so he gave us the tip-off.'

'But how does that work?' asked Styles. 'He'd have to be pretty bloody stupid to send you to the place where he's buried a body, wouldn't he?'

'Maybe we were only supposed to find one body.'

'Yeah, but he's a copper,' argued Styles. 'He would have known there was a good chance you would search the whole area. No, I'm sorry, I don't buy it.'

'Perhaps we were supposed to assume Diana killed them both,' added Watson before reminding Slater, 'you were thinking that way.'

Slater sighed in frustration. 'We need to speak to both of them,' he said, 'because all we've got is supposition. I don't think even Alan Randall can help us much even if he wanted to, and we can't hold him for much longer anyway. Without a confession from someone, we can prove sod all.'

'We need to focus on Diana Randall then,' said Styles, 'because if there's one thing I can tell you for sure, it's that Colin Norton is going nowhere!' He looked at his watch. 'It's five thirty. You two might as well get off. I'll let you know if we find Diana.'

CHAPTER FORTY-ONE

'This case is driving me mad,' said Slater as Watson drove them out of the car park. 'We've got it down to two main suspects and now one of them's in a coma, and the other one's disappeared! Are you with me on this or have I got it completely wrong?'

'I don't think there's much doubt Diana ran down Norton,' said Watson, 'and she must have had a good reason, so I would say it's quite possible, but without some sort of evidence to back it up, it's all just speculation.'

At that moment, Slater's mobile phone began to ring. He fumbled around in his pocket for what seemed like an age, but finally he got it to his ear. The phone was connected to the car by Bluetooth, and Styles' voice boomed in the speakers.

'Slater, it's Styles. Randall's car has just been spotted going into the multi-storey car park at the new shopping centre on the eastern side of town. I've got people closing in as we speak. If you want to make your way over there, you can help us catch her.'

'Fantastic,' said Slater. He took in the solid traffic they were crawling along in. 'We're on the other side of town but we're on our way. We'll get there as quick as we can.'

'Take the ring road,' said Styles, 'it's the quickest way by far at this time of day.'

They were almost on top of the nearest turning onto the ring road, and Watson stamped on the brakes and swung the wheel hard to the left as someone began frantically honking from behind them.

'Sorry about that,' she said, nervously.

'No problem,' said Slater, sounding much more calm than he felt. 'That was quick thinking and it beats trying to find somewhere to turn around in this traffic.'

It took them almost half an hour to crawl the three miles around the ring road so they could come in to town from the eastern side. Slater had been impressed by Watson's composure and patience driving through such heavy traffic, especially after one driver had cut her up for the third time as she was trying to turn off the ring road and into town.

'For God's sake, piss off, you wanker,' she muttered.

It was the first time he'd heard her say anything like that, and Slater couldn't stop himself laughing out loud. Watson seemed to have momentarily forgotten he was there, and she gave him a horrified look when he laughed. 'Oh, goodness, pardon me. I'm so sorry, sir.'

'For goodness' sake, you don't have to apologise for abusing an idiot like that, you were far more polite than I would have been,' he said. 'If we weren't in such a hurry, I'd suggest we pull the guy over and give him an earful.'

'Oh right, well, even so, it's not very professional, is it?'

'It's fine,' said Slater. 'Stop worrying about it. Where's this car park?'

'It's not far, I did a quick recce the day I arrived,' she explained.

'You mean you wanted to know where the best shops are?'

'Well, yes, that as well,' she said, slightly embarrassed. Then she indicated left and turned off the road. 'Here we are.'

A young, harassed-looking uniformed officer was turning angry motorists away from the barrier and waved frantically at Watson as she ignored his signals to turn away. She pressed a button and her window glided down as she pulled up next to him.

'Can't you see me waving at you?' he snapped, angrily.

'Of course I can,' she said, giving him a winning smile and waving her warrant card at him. 'DS Brearley and DI Slater,' she said. 'I think we're expected.'

He looked at the card, but it was her smile that won him over. 'Oh, right, yes, miss, I'm sorry.'

'That's all right, officer,' she said. 'I know how frustrating it can be. We've all been there.'

The young PC opened the barrier for her. 'They're ten floors up, on the roof,' he said.

'Thank you,' said Watson and gave him another smile for good measure as she drove past him and headed towards the first ramp.

'Did I detect the use of your female charms there, Watson?' asked Slater. He could see she was smiling to herself as she negotiated the successive turns.

'It doesn't cost anything to share a smile,' she said. 'He's probably going to get nothing but abuse for the next few hours turning people away from this car park, but now at least one person has given him a smile.'

'I'm sure you're right,' said Slater, 'and I suspect you've just made his night.'

'Sometimes you just have to use what you've got to get what you want,' said Watson. 'And most men like a nice smile.'

On another occasion, such a remark may well have piqued Slater's curiosity, but right now they had more pressing matters to attend to. 'I've got a bad feeling about this,' he said. 'Can you think of more than one reason why she would want to be up on the roof?'

'Do you think she's going to jump?'

'I bloody well hope not,' he said, 'but can you think of any other reason for her to be up there?'

'Have you had to deal with a jumper before?' she asked.

'No, but it's probably just as well, I'm not much good with heights.'

'So, that's tunnels, boats and heights,' she said.

He turned to look at her, and there was just the hint of a smile about her face. 'Yes, and your point is?'

'They say you should get up close to your phobias and face up to them if you want to overcome them,' she said.

'Yes, thank you for your advice,' he said, rather more tetchily than he intended. 'I'll bear that in mind. Perhaps next time we take a ferry we can re-enact the scene where they're up at the bow of the *Titanic*.'

'The *Titanic*'s probably not the best choice for a re-enactment if you're not keen on wa—'

Watson's sentence was cut short by the dirty look Slater aimed in her direction.

Nothing more was said as they zoomed up and around the final two ramps and emerged onto the roof. The immediate area had been cordoned off. There was enough room for two or three vehicles, and the remaining space was crammed with what appeared to be a small army of police officers. Beyond the cordon, the roof seemed to stretch a long way off into the distance. A hastily erected searchlight revealed a tiny figure in silhouette, apparently suspended in mid-air beyond the wall that surrounded the roof.

DI Styles elbowed his way through the crowd towards them as Slater and Watson climbed from the car. The crowd turned as one, expectant faces filling in the space all around Styles. They were nowhere near the edge of the roof but even so, Slater was already beginning to feel distinctly edgy.

'We've got a problem,' said Styles, anxiously, as he reached them. 'She says she's going to jump.'

'There you are, Watson,' said Slater, flippantly. 'I told you she hadn't come up here to enjoy the view.'

Styles looked like he wasn't quite sure what to say to that.

'So why doesn't she jump if that's what she wants to do?' said Slater, irritably. 'What's she waiting for?'

'She says she wants to talk.'

'Well, what are you waiting for? Get a negotiator out here and talk her down.'

'That's what we're going to do,' said Styles, patiently. 'We've just been waiting for him to arrive.'

'Well, how much longer is he going to be?'

'He's here now,' said Styles, ominously.

Slater took a moment to catch up. 'Now, just a minute, I hope you're not suggesting—'

'Yes, it's you,' said Styles with a half-smile. 'She won't speak to anyone else.'

Slater's face turned ashen. 'Yeah, well, you can forget that bloody idea straight away,' he said. 'I get dizzy looking out of an upstairs window. I'm not standing on the edge of a roof ten bloody floors up.'

'I'll go,' said Watson.

'I can't let you do that,' said Styles. 'She says she'll only talk to DI Slater. She's made it quite clear if we send anyone else near her, she'll jump.'

'What makes you so sure she'll do it?' asked Slater.

'You can never be sure,' said Styles, 'but when we got here she was just sitting on the wall. When one of my men went over to try and talk to her, she climbed over. Right now, she's perched on a narrow ledge less than a foot wide with an arm draped over the wall. If she lets go of that wall, she's a goner, and she says if anyone other than you comes within ten yards, that's exactly what she's going to do.'

'Well, that's up to her, isn't it?' said Slater, callously.

Styles glanced down and an embarrassed Slater realised he had noticed his shaking hands. 'You know as well as me that it doesn't work like that,' he said, gently. 'It's my duty, as lead officer, to try and stop her from jumping. She's given us a possible way out. I'm sorry, Slater, but it's got to be you. We'll fit you up with a microphone and earpiece so we'll be in touch all the time.'

'What is it you expect me to do?'

'Whatever you can to get her to come down,' said Styles.

Slater thought about it. As the conversation had gone on, the faces around them had turned from expectant to neutral and were now heading towards hostile as they waited for his decision. He let out a huge sigh. He knew Styles was right. He had no choice. 'All right, I'll do it,' he said, reluctantly.

As he turned to Watson, he could hear the murmurs of approval from the small crowd. 'Is this going to be getting up close enough to my phobias for you?' he hissed.

'I think it's very brave of you,' she said.

'I don't want to be bloody brave. I just want to be safe.'

'I'm coming with you as back up' she said.

'That's a great idea,' he agreed, with a wry smile. 'You can carry the spare underpants. I've got a feeling I'll be needing them.'

CHAPTER FORTY-TWO

'Is that you, Slater?' Diana had been watching as they approached, and they were about ten yards away when she called out to them.

'Yes.'

'Okay, you can stop right there. Is that DS Brearley with you? I said you were to come alone.'

'I was told you said no one else within ten yards. If it's a problem, I can send her back.'

He watched anxiously as Diana mulled this over. 'No, she can stay now she's here,' she said, finally, 'but she doesn't come any closer. In fact, she can go and sit on the wall over there.' She pointed away to her left, and Slater realised she wanted Watson where she could keep an eye on her.

'I don't think that's a good idea,' said Watson, quietly.

'Nor is pissing her off,' said Slater. 'We'll never find out what happened if she jumps now.'

'Yes, but what about you?'

'I'll be fine,' said Slater.

'Are you sure?'

'No, but do it anyway.'

'Yes, but—'

'Sam, don't make me start ordering you about,' said Slater. 'Just do it.'

'That was very touching,' said Diana, sarcastically. 'Now do as he says.'

Reluctantly, Watson made her way to the wall where Diana had pointed. 'Don't stop there,' said Diana, 'I want to see you sitting on the wall. You won't be able to do anything foolish if you're balancing up there.'

Slater watched as Watson carefully eased herself up and shuffled round so she was sitting on the wall. He was feeling distinctly queasy now and wondered how he was going to cope if Diana wanted him to do the same.

'That's better,' said Diana, 'now you stay there. If I see you so much as move, I'll jump, got it?' Then she turned her attention back to Slater. 'She cares about you, Slater. Isn't that nice? But if you take my advice you'll be very careful, these workplace romances really aren't a good idea.'

'Are we going to shout at each other from long range or are you going to let me near enough to talk?' asked Slater.

'You can come closer,' she said, 'but first I want to see you ditch your microphone and earpiece.'

'No!' hissed Styles in Slater's ear. 'You can't do that. We need to hear what's going on.'

'He's right,' agreed Watson.

Slater hesitated. Should he do as she asked?

'I'm waiting,' warned Diana. 'You're not going to find your answers if I jump now.'

Slater reached for his earpiece. As soon as he moved, Styles was shouting in his ear. 'Slater! I forbid you to remove that equipment.'

'You said to do whatever I can to get her down,' Slater said into his microphone, as he tossed the earpiece to one side, 'so that's what I'm doing.' He tugged the microphone from his collar, held it up so Diana could clearly see it, and then threw it after the earpiece.

'That's better,' she said approvingly. 'Now you can come over here, but don't think you're going to try any heroics.'

'Don't worry,' he said, as he took his first steps towards her. 'Heroics and heights just aren't my thing.'

Diana watched, fascinated, as Slater came closer. Then she seemed to realise how terrified he was. 'Come right up to the wall,' she said invitingly, a broad smile on her face. She pointed to a spot a few feet from where she was.

'This is fine,' Slater said, 'I can hear you from here.'

'That wasn't a request,' she hissed.

'Oh, crap, really?' he asked. 'Do I have to?'

'I know you're a bit scared—' she said.

'A bit scared? Who me?' he said. 'I'm not a bit scared, I'm bloody terrified!'

'The thing to do with your fears—'

'Is to face up to them, yes I know,' said Slater, glancing across at Watson. 'So I've been told.'

'Well, then,' said Diana. 'Come and look over the wall.'

'I'd rather not.'

Diana was still holding onto the wall, but she leaned away from it, just long enough to make her point.

'All right, all right,' said Slater, hastily. 'Don't jump. I'll do it.'

He shuffled agonisingly towards the wall. By the time he reached it he was sweating profusely and shaking uncontrollably. He grabbed the top of the wall and clung to it, eyes closed tight.

'It's such a shame it's dark,' she said. 'You can see my old house from up here.'

'Oh, dear, what a pity we're going to miss it,' said Slater, his voice almost unrecognisable.

'Open your eyes,' she said.

Slater slowly opened his eyes, making sure to keep his gaze on Diana's face.

'Now look down there.' She pointed down towards the ground, and obediently he allowed his gaze to follow, finally going up on tiptoes to see right over. He had turned a deathly shade of white and now his head began to swim and he gagged a couple of times.

'Careful,' said Diana, not unkindly. 'I don't want another death on my conscience.'

* * *

Ten yards away, Watson had Styles ranting in her ear. 'Has he pulled off his back-up mike as well?'

'I don't think so,' she whispered.

'Well, I hope you can hear the conversation then,' he snapped, angrily, 'because the bloody thing isn't working.'

'I might be able to hear better if you stop shouting in my ear,' muttered Watson, but she had only managed to catch the odd word since Slater had reached Diana, so she didn't hold out much hope.

'I heard that, DS Brearley,' raged Styles. 'I'll remind you I'm the senior officer here.'

'Yes, sir,' said Watson, 'I understand that, but it's actually DI Slater who's risking his life here, and if the mike's not working it's not his fault and it's not mine. I respectfully suggest shouting in my ear isn't helping.'

'I'll deal with you later, Brearley.'

* * *

Meanwhile, Slater's legs seemed to have turned to rubber, and he could hear the blood pounding in his head as his heart began racing. He was now using the wall to stop himself from collapsing in an undignified heap. He wondered how much longer he could keep this up.

'Take some deep breaths,' said Diana, a trace of concern in her voice. 'You'll feel much better.'

He did as she suggested, and after a short while, his head stopped spinning and he began to calm down.

'I suppose you've worked it all out now, haven't you?' she suddenly asked.

Slater felt the urge to tell her that actually no, he hadn't, but he had several theories if she could just give him some pointers. He resisted the urge, however, and said nothing.

'I never meant to kill anyone, you know?' she said.

'But you ran Colin Norton down,' argued Slater. 'We've got a witness who saw you accelerate straight at him.'

'Oh, I meant to kill *him*,' she said matter-of-factly. 'But he deserved to die. It was all his fault. None of this would have happened if I'd never met him.'

Slater wondered if he should tell her Colin Norton wasn't actually dead, but he decided to keep it to himself for now. He was more interested in finding out what she could tell him about the bodies.

'But why did you want to kill Colin?' asked Slater. 'I thought you were lovers?'

'Ha! That was a long time ago,' she said scornfully. 'It was the biggest mistake of my life. I thought I'd got away from him when I went to Flipton, but he knew what I'd done. He used it against me. I was trapped.'

'He was blackmailing you?'

'Yes, but not in the way you think of blackmail. He was using me for sex, not money,' she said. 'He insisted we had to carry on with our affair or he'd tell everyone what I had done. I would have lost everything.'

Slater couldn't quite believe what he was hearing. 'He was blackmailing you for *sex*?'

'Can you imagine? It was like agreeing to be raped every week. And then he started to come to our house like some long-lost friend, and of course, Alan invited him in, and I had to pretend . . .'

She seemed to be genuinely distressed at this point, so Slater gave her a few moments to compose herself. While he waited, he thought about what he'd just heard. They had suspected blackmail was involved somehow, and they had suspected Diana had still been seeing Norton, but this scenario had never crossed their minds. He glanced towards Watson, but in the poor light he couldn't see her face clearly. He just hoped Styles had enabled her earpiece so she could hear what Diana was saying.

'I used to spend half of every Wednesday night in the shower, I felt so dirty,' Diana continued. 'He always used to tell me I had brought it on myself, but it was his fault right from the beginning.'

She said nothing for what seemed like an age, and Slater began to think that was all she was going to tell him, so he took a wild guess. 'So he was there the night you ran Kylie down?'

'I had ended the affair a couple of weeks before,' she said. 'I saw the move to Flipton as a chance to get away from him and start over. Alan's a good man, you know? He didn't deserve to have me cheating on him. I wanted to put that right, but Norton was threatening to tell Alan if we didn't have one last night together.'

She gave Slater a knowing look. 'Yes, I know, you're thinking how bloody stupid am I? A trained detective inspector, and I actually thought he would go away if I gave him what he wanted.'

'I wasn't thinking that,' said Slater. 'I was just wondering if I would have done any different if I was in that situation. I think if desperation offered us an easy path, most of us would take it. Isn't that what panic does?'

'I was a bloody fool.'

There was another long silence.

'So this was the night of your leaving party?' asked Slater.

'There's a hotel we used to go to,' she explained. 'It's far enough away for us to be anonymous. We used to go there a lot.'

'And you had to drive through Trillington to get there?'

'Yes, that's right.'

'And what happened? Were you drunk?'

'Good God, no,' she said. 'I'd had a couple, and I would have failed a breathalyser, but drunk? No way.'

'We figured maybe you'd come up behind Kylie Mason, lost control, and run her down.'

'Oh, I lost control all right,' she said, 'but only because that animal Norton couldn't keep his bloody hands to himself. It's a bit difficult to keep your car under control when someone suddenly shoves his hand between your legs!'

Slater thought he couldn't argue with that. 'So you ran her down?'

'I tried to avoid her, but the road was damp and the car went into a skid . . .' She stopped for a few moments. 'We ended up going broadside. It was the back end of the car that hit her. Once I realised what I'd done, I just screamed at Norton to get out of the car and run. I couldn't afford to have anyone find us in that situation so I told him I would sort it out, and if anyone asked anything, we were never there.'

Slater felt a brief satisfaction as a gap in their theory about what had happened had just been filled. 'So you actually wanted to keep him out of it? That sounds like you cared about him.'

'Don't be ridiculous,' she said, scornfully. 'It was damage limitation.'

Now it was Slater's turn to be scornful. 'Even in a situation like that, the only thing you were worried about was yourself? My God, Diana, what a piece of work you are!'

She looked daggers at him, and then looked down to the ground below her. For a moment, Slater's blood ran cold as he thought she was going to jump.

'If you're supposed to be talking me down,' she said, 'I don't think abusing me is the approved method.'

'I should warn you I've not done the training,' admitted Slater, 'so I'm making this up as I go along. I should also warn you, all I'm really interested in is solving my case and saving my own skin.'

'And I should warn you this is my confession,' said Diana, 'but I've no intention of going to prison.'

Slater knew exactly what she was suggesting, but he was shocked to find he didn't much care if she jumped. He wondered where this new callous streak had come from, then quickly remembered his situation. Of course he didn't much care about her; it was her fault he was hanging onto this bloody wall in fear of his life, and that's what was dictating his feelings.

He took a deep breath and decided he wouldn't be able to keep this up for much longer. He needed to get things moving.

'And then what happened?'

'Once he had run for his life, I got out of the car. It was deathly quiet. I went to the girl, but there was no pulse. I couldn't do anything for her.'

'What about the baby she was carrying? She had only gone out to try and get him to sleep!'

'I didn't know she was carrying a baby at first. It was only when I started to roll her towards the ditch that the baby started crying. I would have lost my licence, and my job, and my husband . . .'

'So you decided it would be all right to steal the baby and shove his mother into a ditch and forget about her,' suggested Slater.

'It wasn't like that,' snapped Diana.

'Oh, but of course it was,' said Slater. 'All you cared about was covering your arse. Did you ever think about that girl's family? What about her boyfriend? Did you know who he was?'

She said nothing.

'Ah, but of course you did, didn't you? I bet Colin Norton called you as soon as the guy came in and started asking questions.'

'That's where you're wrong,' she said. 'Norton never mentioned Hudson.'

'I find that hard to believe,' said Slater. 'A year or so later, he was living on the farm right next to your house. You even socialised with him!'

'That was purely coincidental. When we moved in next to the major, Hudson wasn't living there yet. Then later all we knew was the man had served under the major, and he had moved into the cottage on the farm because he was working there. We only found out much later that he'd done time, but even then we didn't know why, and he didn't talk about it so we didn't ask.' She could see Slater was unconvinced. 'I promise you I had no idea who he was.'

Slater thought this part of her story was highly unlikely, but he knew he couldn't prove it one way or the other.

'At least now I understand why Norton didn't take Hudson seriously when he reported Kylie missing,' he said. 'So, not only did the poor guy lose his girlfriend and baby, but he got six months and a prison record, all because of you!'

'It was Norton's fault, not mine!' she snapped.

'No, Diana, the decision to get involved with Norton was yours, and yours alone. Anything that happened as a consequence of that was a result of you making that choice.'

There was a stony silence as Slater's words faded into the ether.

'Hudson never knew your Sonny was actually his son, did he?' asked Slater. 'He even helped with the searches, didn't he? How ironic is that? How could you do that to the poor man?'

Diana said nothing for a minute or two. Slater thought that was quite appropriate, after all, what could she say really?

'I suppose you know I had an abortion?' asked Diana, eventually.

'Yes, we guessed that must have been Norton's baby.'

'I'd never even thought about having a baby before and getting rid of it wasn't difficult, but then soon after I began to realise just how much I wanted to have one. I even turned one of our bedrooms into a nursery so that it would be ready if I ever got pregnant.'

'Yet you had told Alan you couldn't have children.'

'Yes, that was a stupid thing for me to do,' she admitted. 'It certainly complicated things. But then, quite unexpectedly, I found Sonny, and he had no mother to look after him and love him, so taking him home just seemed to be the right thing to do.'

Slater had been starting to think Diana was perhaps a little disturbed, but now he was becoming convinced she was more than a little bit. 'Where does Alan come into all this?' he asked. 'It's not as if you can hide a baby. He must have known what you'd done.'

'He was away when it happened. When he got back, the baby was already there. He knew how much I wanted a baby and we'd always agreed that he would be a stay-at-home dad so I could carry on with my career. We agreed that if anyone ever asked, we would say we'd adopted the baby.'

'So he turned a blind eye to the fact you'd killed someone and taken their baby?'

'It's not his fault,' she said. 'He did it for me.'

'Oh, that's all right then,' muttered Slater, bitterly, before adding, 'So, let's move on to when Sonny disappeared.'

'That was the worst day of my life,' she said. 'I died inside that day. I'd never known what depression was, but it's been there with me ever since.'

'So leaving the job because of depression was a load of crap?'

She sighed. 'I told Norton I wasn't going to be blackmailed any more, so he sent an anonymous letter to my chief constable about me having an affair with a junior officer. The CC made it clear I had to go, but at least he was prepared to lie about why.'

'But you carried on seeing Norton?'

'He told me next time he would tell everyone about the body in the ditch. What else could I do?'

'So, who took Sonny?' asked Slater. 'At one point we thought it might have been you or Alan.'

Diana looked horrified. 'How could you possibly think that? We loved him.'

'So who do you think took him?' asked Slater.

'I always suspected Norton,' said Diana, 'but there was never any proof. I always knew that if I ever found out who had done it, I would kill that person. When I heard Ramlinstoke had been given a tip-off about a body in a ditch, I was confident it was the girl's body and there was a good chance no one would ever connect her to me, but then when you came to see me about finding Sonny, I knew it could only have been one person behind all of it.'

Another penny dropped for Slater. 'Of course,' he said. 'Norton was the only other person who knew you'd pushed Kylie Mason's body into that ditch, but why did he have to kill Sonny?'

'Only he can answer that,' she said, 'but I suspect it was to punish me because I refused to play his game any more.'

'Why wait ten years before the tip-off?'

'Again, you'd have to ask him. But I can tell you he never stopped contacting me over the years, telling me I had to see him or else. I used to keep changing my mobile number, but then he'd turn up at our house, like the good friend Alan thought he was. I gave up in the end and took the calls without speaking. It used to annoy the hell out of him so at least I got some small satisfaction from that.'

'But he must have known we'd find Sonny's body as well as Kylie's,' said Slater.

'Of course he knew, but he doesn't care. He's got a brain tumour and barely six months to live. The important thing for him was that it would lead you to me.'

'He could have just told us.'

'I think he wanted to see me suffer slowly as you put it all together.'

'So he's been calling you with updates just to make sure you knew we were closing in?'

'That's about the size of it,' she said, holding Slater's gaze. 'I knew from the first day you came to see us that you wouldn't let it go until you worked it all out.'

She stared into space for what seemed like an age to Slater, but in reality was no more than thirty seconds. 'I'm not really a bad person, you know,' she said, finally. 'I could have really been someone and had it all, but instead I made a complete mess of everything. This is going to ruin Alan's life when he learns everything I've done.'

* * *

Still perched on the wall, Watson heard the slight click in her ear, but this time, instead of another rant, the voice was much calmer. 'This is Styles. I've just been informed Colin Norton has passed away. I thought you should know.'

'Right, sir, thank you. I'll tell DI Slater when I get a chance.'

* * *

Diana had been sidling closer to Slater, who was still clinging grimly to the wall, and now she was almost directly in front of him, with just the wall between them.

'Will you hold me?' she said. 'I think I've had enough of this now.'

Slater really didn't want to let go of the wall, but if this was a chance to get a hold of her, he couldn't ignore it. 'Of course,' he said and reached his arms around her shoulders as she slipped hers around his neck and rested her head on his shoulder.

They stood like this for a minute or so, like two awkward lovers after something had come between them, in this case a four-and-a-half-foot wall.

'We'd be a lot more comfortable if this damned wall wasn't in the way,' said Slater.

Diana leaned her head back so she was looking into Slater's eyes, just inches away. She gave him a beautiful smile. 'Why, Detective Inspector, what are you suggesting?' she said with a twinkle in her eye. 'Are you going to come and join me?'

Slater peered over the side, and closed his eyes as nausea threatened to take control again. 'I just think you should climb back over this side,' he said, looking back into Diana's eyes.

'You know you're right,' she said. 'I really should, shouldn't I? But you'll need to give me a bit of room, won't you?'

He studied her face. Was she for real? He was trying to figure out how he could give her some space and keep hold of her when she suddenly reached her face up to his and gave him the softest peck on the lips. Slater was momentarily so surprised he relaxed his hold of her, and in that instant she smiled, whispered, 'Thank you,' and stepped back off the ledge.

'Diana! No!' Desperately, Slater scrambled onto the wall, reaching out for her, but she was gone. He looked over the edge and watched in horror as her body tumbled from sight. There was an eerie silence followed by a dull thud as Diana hit the ground below. He stared vacantly down into the darkness, quite unaware of the figures running towards him or of Watson holding onto his legs, trying to drag him down off the wall.

* * *

FOUR DAYS LATER

David Hudson's French wife, Monique, had contacted Watson the day after Diana Randall had jumped to her death, to ask if she could bring her husband over to ensure the bodies were given proper burials. Watson had explained to her that all that remained were bones, and she wasn't sure how soon they would be released, but had agreed to Monique's request that it would be good for him to come over and visit the scene of Kylie's death. After years of wondering what had really happened, it should at least give him some closure.

Now, as they stood together staring at the excavation site, Watson thought that for such a big man David Hudson looked remarkably small and almost child-like as he stood and stared at the excavation site, clutching Monique's hand, rather like a small boy might cling to his mother.

'And she actually died here?' he asked Watson. 'Two police officers ran her down, pushed her into that ditch and just drove off and left her?'

'I'm afraid so,' said Watson, feeling somehow responsible by association. 'Diana Randall told DI Slater it was very dark that night, and she lost control of her car and that's how she came to hit Kylie.'

'So, she says it was an accident?'

'We'll never know for sure, of course, but we've found nothing to suggest otherwise, so we believe she was telling the truth.'

'That's not much consolation, is it?'

'It's no consolation at all,' agreed Watson. She wanted to say more, but felt whatever she said would be inadequate.

'All those years I lived a stone's throw from that woman's house,' said Hudson. 'I'm sure I recall I even kicked a football around with Sonny at the major's house once . . .' He fell silent briefly as he choked back a sob. 'And all that time I never knew he was my own son, or that she had killed his mother.'

His wife tightened her grip on his hand, stroked his arm reassuringly, and spoke quietly to him. 'Be strong,' she said. 'You need to do this. Trust me, you will feel better afterwards. At least now they have paid for what they did, and you can stop wondering what happened.'

'I've spoken to the authorities,' said Watson. 'Now that everyone has agreed who was responsible for what happened, and as those two people are now dead, there will be no trial, so I've asked for the bodies to be released as soon as possible.'

'Do you know when that will be?' asked Monique.

'I think it will be in a couple of days. There are just a couple of formalities to clear up. It's just paperwork really. I can let you know as soon as I know.'

'We're going up to see the major for a few days while we're over here,' said Hudson. 'Monique's never met him, and I haven't seen him for years.'

'You've been in touch, then?' asked Watson.

'I think I owed him that,' said Hudson. 'I should have kept in contact with him, he was very good to me. We're going to try and build some bridges.'

'I'm sure you will,' said Watson. 'He seems like a very decent man.'

'One of the best,' said Hudson. 'He's pretty confident he can persuade his local vicar to conduct the funerals.'

'Have you decided what you're going to do?'

'Cremation,' said Hudson. He looked fondly at his wife. 'Monique suggested it. This way we can take the ashes back to France with us. I know Kylie would have loved France, and we think where we live is the perfect place for a little boy.'

* * *

ONE WEEK LATER

'Hi, Norm, it's Sam,' said Watson.

'Oh hi,' said Norman. 'If you want to speak to Dave, he's sleeping right now, and I really don't wanna wake him.'

'No, that's okay, how is he?'

'Not great. He looks like he hasn't slept more than a couple of minutes this last week. He says every time he shuts his eyes, he sees Diana smiling at him as she steps back off that ledge.'

'It wasn't his fault,' said Watson. 'She had intended to do that all along.'

'Yeah, but he blames himself for getting close enough to have a hold of her and then letting go at the vital moment.'

'She conned him,' said Watson.

'You know it, and I know it,' said Norman, 'but none of that matters if he doesn't accept it.'

'It wouldn't be so bad, but even her confession counts for nothing because he was the only one who heard it, and the only guy who could have confirmed any of it died in hospital.'

'Yeah, I know. It's tough, but that's life,' said Norman. 'Shit happens.'

'He needs Jenny,' said Watson. 'Has she come back yet?'

Norman sighed. 'No sign of her so far,' he said, 'but Dave doesn't seem worried about it. He tells me they had been arguing almost every night while he was away. He thinks she might even have left him.'

'What do you think?'

'Honestly? I have to admit I'm concerned. I've been poking around while he's asleep, and if she has left him, she hasn't taken much of her stuff with her. And if I know Jenny, she wouldn't just walk out like that. Don't take this the wrong way, I do like her, but she does like to be the centre of attention, and she does like a drama. She's the sort who would take the scissors to his clothes, but there's no sign of anything like that. I'm sure, if she was going to leave him, she would have waited until he came back and then made a really big deal out of the whole thing.'

Watson didn't have time to speak before Norman continued.

'And another thing, Dave says she mentioned going to see her parents. As far as I know she burnt her bridges with them a long, long time ago. Something about this whole situation doesn't seem right to me, but I don't want to worry him. He's got enough to deal with right now.'

'You said he doesn't seem worried.'

'I probably didn't put that right. It's like he's almost unaware of what's going on around him. I think he's been so affected by what happened, he's still in shock, and those stupid pills they've given him don't help. They just seem to make his brain go numb, that's why he sleeps so much.'

'She could call,' said Watson, her annoyance clear. 'Surely if she knew what had happened she would be there for him even if they had fallen out?'

'Well, that's another thing that worries me,' said Norman. 'I've tried calling her at all times of the day and night, but her damned phone's always switched off.'

'That's not helping anyone, is it?'

'Of course not, but it's a good way of making sure you don't have to talk to anyone,' said Norman. 'There again, maybe I'm being unfair and she's lost her phone somehow.'

'But he needs someone there to look after him, and help get him over this.'

'Yeah, well, I'm not exactly rushed off my feet right now, so I've moved in for a few days.'

'But you're still supposed to be resting and recuperating from your heart attack!'

'I am resting and I'm keeping an eye on him too. It's not difficult because he's not exactly Mr High Energy at the moment, he's more like Mr Zombie. I'm having to bully him into going out for a walk with me every day, but he's only doing it because he thinks it's for my benefit. Really it's as much for him as it is for me.'

'I've been told he's been signed off work for another month. He can't come back until he's passed the psych evaluation.'

'That's normal after a major traumatic event,' Norman assured her. 'We'll get him through it, he just needs some time, that's all.'

'I wouldn't rush him if I were you,' warned Watson. 'I think they might be preparing a lamb for the slaughter.'

'What?'

'I've heard nothing official,' she said, 'but from what I've managed to overhear, there's going to be an inquiry.'

'That's crazy! What's he supposed to have done?'

'They're saying he was wrong to remove his microphone and earpiece, and they're blaming him for the back-up microphone not working.'

'If equipment doesn't work that's a tech problem, not his,' said Norman.

'It gets worse,' said Watson. 'There's even a suggestion he didn't try to stop her from jumping.'

'That is total bullshit,' said Norman. 'He would never have stood back and let her jump!'

'He didn't. I was there, I saw what happened, and I'm going to make sure I get the opportunity to tell them.'

'Jeez, I hope you're wrong about this. Look, whatever's going on, I don't think he needs to hear about it right now, so please don't mention it if you speak to him, huh?'

'Don't worry, I won't say a word about it,' she promised. 'I have to go now, but there is one bit of good news you can tell him.'

'Oh, yeah, what's that?' asked Norman.

'I've heard on the grapevine that the local police have been investigating Colin Norton's affairs and they've found a link between him and Howard Glossop.'

'That's the sleazy landlord guy who tried to get a sly grope, right?'

'That's him,' confirmed Watson. 'The word is Norton was supplying him with dirty videos that had been confiscated as evidence. Apparently they've interviewed Glossop's wife and she's been more than happy to spill the beans on several little scams he's involved in.'

'Ha! Maybe there is some sort of justice after all,' said Norman.

'Tell Dave when he wakes up, it might cheer him up a little. Tell him I called, will you? And if there's anything I can do just let me know. When he's feeling up to it, let me know, and I'll come and see him.'

'I'll be sure to tell him you called,' said Norman, 'and thanks for thinking of him.'

'He's a nice man,' said Watson. 'He risked his life for Diana, he certainly didn't deserve to have her do this to him.'

'Yeah, he is a nice guy,' said Norman, 'but life has a habit of kicking nice guys in the teeth, right?'

As Watson hung up, she thought about Jenny's disappearance and what Norman had just said about his concerns. She just hoped he was wrong.

THE END

THE JOFFE BOOKS STORY

We began in 2014 when Jasper agreed to publish his mum's much-rejected romance novel and it became a bestseller.

Since then we've grown into the largest independent publisher in the UK. We're extremely proud to publish some of the very best writers in the world, including Joy Ellis, Faith Martin, Caro Ramsay, Helen Forrester, Simon Brett and Robert Goddard. Everyone at Joffe Books loves reading and we never forget that it all begins with the magic of an author telling a story.

We are proud to publish talented first-time authors, as well as established writers whose books we love introducing to a new generation of readers.

We won Trade Publisher of the Year at the Independent Publishing Awards in 2023. We have been shortlisted for Independent Publisher of the Year at the British Book Awards for the last four years, and were shortlisted for the Diversity and Inclusivity Award at the 2022 Independent Publishing Awards. In 2023 we were shortlisted for Publisher of the Year at the RNA Industry Awards.

We built this company with your help, and we love to hear from you, so please email us about absolutely anything bookish at feedback@joffebooks.com

If you want to receive free books every Friday and hear about all our new releases, join our mailing list: www.joffebooks.com/contact

And when you tell your friends about us, just remember: it's pronounced Joffe as in coffee or toffee!

ALSO BY P.F. FORD

SLATER AND NORMAN MYSTERIES
Book 1: DEATH BY CARPET
Book 2: DEATH BY PLANE
Book 3: DEATH BY NIGHT
Book 4: DEATH BY KITCHEN SINK
Book 5: DEATH BY TELEPHONE BOX
Book 6: DEATH IN WILD BOAR WOODS
Book 7: DEATH IN THE RIVER
Book 8: DEATH IN A SKIP
Book 9: DEATH OF A PENSIONER
Book 10: DEATH OF A LONG-LOST SON

THE WEST WALES MURDER MYSTERIES
Prequel: A DATE WITH DEATH
Book 1: A BODY ON THE BEACH
Book 2: A BODY OUT AT SEA
Book 3: A BODY DOWN THE LANE
Book 4: A BODY AT THE FARMHOUSE
Book 5: A BODY IN THE COTTAGE

Made in United States
North Haven, CT
10 August 2024

55868595R00136